For our first gran

Claudia Dixon

who loves her two moggie stable cats
'*Whisky*' and '*Cola*'
and greatly admires our sophisticated
Maine Coon cat
'*Batty*'

Inscribed by the author
Jeremy Mallinson

C O N T E N T S

Chapter One

Parkington Hall

I t was in the head groom's quarters above the main coach house that Fantasia first encountered the campaign-scarred Nevasta. A year previously, such a meeting would have taken place at the Hall itself; but ever since the young Lady Stocksfield had arrived with her Irish wolf-hounds, Fantasia and her attendants had had to discreetly withdraw from the Hall, and take up residence in the comparative safety of the nearby stable-yard.

Fantasia was a remarkably sophisticated cat, coming as she did from one of the oldest lines of chinchilla Persians, which had itself originated from silver tabby cat stock. Her large, round and expressive emerald-coloured eyes contrasted magnificently with the brick-red patch of the end of her snub nose. Her broad head was plumed by small but well-tufted ears, which both appeared to react independently to every noise that occurred. Her chubby body, supported by short thick legs, was finished off neatly by an impressive bushy tail tipped, as were her ears, with black. Her chinchilla-coloured coat was long and dense but silky and fine in texture and the purity of colour of her 'snowdrop' white undercoat lacked any signs of the yellow tinges displayed so frequently by cats of less aristocratic stock.

As Nevasta entered the room, Fantasia and her three chinchilla Persian companions sprang to their feet, arching their backs like croquet hoops and, with tails erect, hissed their displeasure at the unannounced intruder; warning him not to take one step further without first stating his business and the reason for his unheralded presence. Unaccustomed as Nevasta was to taking any notice of such a challenge, he found himself temporarily mesmerised by the striking, dignified appearance of these long-hair felines; in particular with the presence of the regal bearing of Fantasia.

Nevasta had had a very different type of background from Fantasia, possessing none of the aristocratic qualities of a true pedigree; but in its place he had adopted the arrogant countenance of a successful bandit, who took delight in informing his associates as to just how exceedingly common his ancestry was. He had been born just over eight years previously in one of the narrow alleys off the back streets of Menton on the Cote d'Azur in Southern France. Whilst searching for food one day, he had been picked up as a stray and conveyed, entangled in a net, to the palatial residence of Count Dominic de Demburn on Cap Martin who, over the years, had gone out of his way to provide a home for what he considered to be the waifs and strays and the deprived starving cats of the region.

At the time of Nevasta's arrival at Chateau Santa Sophia, there had been some eighty-six cats of just about every shape, colour and size in residence, the only common denominator between them being that they had all come from what the Count considered to be the underprivileged side of the life of domestic cats. But in spite of the cats' new-found palatial home with the Count, they were for ever shunned by the pedigree cats of that region. It had taken Nevasta almost six years to battle his way to the top of the Count's cat kingdom, during which time he had had to rely on all of his instincts and wits in order to produce the type of cunning, intrigue and strategy, that had earned him his present elevated position as the king figure of the tribe of some one hundred and twenty waifs and strays.

It had been a tough climb to the summit, for he had had not only to fight his way through many a domestic campaign, becoming battle-scarred in the process, but also had had to cultivate the quality of being able to charm his adversaries and mature as a good diplomat, so that a lasting relationship of mutual respect with the Count could be secured. This he had now accomplished to such a degree that, whenever the Count travelled abroad, he insisted that Nevasta accompanied him. The Count likened this to a Head of State always electing to travel with his Prime Minister.

Nevasta was, by any standards, a large cat, whose tiger-striped ginger body was supported by sturdy long legs, which were well furred down to his plate-like paws. Each foot displayed an armoury of needle-sharp claws at the end, with an underside of hard, pinkish scaled pads. His head was square, his slant-set greyish eyes were large and staring and his erect, cavernous ears were as alert as radar receivers. His nose resembled a rose-pink triangle leading to a mouth that curved downwards, with lips that could hardly conceal his long, ivory-like teeth. From each side of his cheeks sprouted generous sets of bristly white whiskers that would put any shaving brush to shame. A ginger stripe ran along the top of his back before giving way to the ginger and greyish rings of his white-plumed tail. A nick out of his left ear and a partly closed right eye were his only battle scars. But whatever way Nevasta was regarded, he possessed the presence and charisma of both a warrior and a leader.

These were still the days of gracious living and, as the automobile had only recently become quite a common sight, the majority of people either travelled by train or went by other public transport. However, as far as the Count was concerned, there was now only one way to travel, and that was by way of his massive 1925 3-litre Bentley. It was therefore by this fashion that he had journeyed with Nevasta the thousand miles or so from Cap Martin, on the sun-drenched shores of the Mediterranean, to the smokey-grey of the North of England, in order to spend a short holiday with his old university friend, Lord Stocksfield.

On their arrival at Parkington Hall, the Count had been rather put out when he realised that, due to the new Lady Stocksfield's cat-hating Irish wolf-hounds, Nevasta would for his own safety have to stay elsewhere. Dogs were not allowed back on the Count's own property and, previously, when he had stayed at a place which supported dogs, Nevasta had always been able to hold his own and even put some breeds to flight. But alas, it had been a very different matter when Nevasta had brushed past the Stocksfields into the great hall in order to inspect it. A grey shaggy shape, almost the size of a small pony, had dashed out from under the great staircase, snarling most inhospitably as it advanced and, had it not been for the slipperiness of the marble floor - which caused the wolf-hound, in its anxiety to get at Nevasta, to skid off course - Nevasta was almost certain that his days would have come to an end. Fortunately, Nevasta was able to make good his escape, taking the precaution of leaping back into the safety of the Count's Bentley where, burning with indignation, he awaited

'Fantasia' with 'Nevasta' at Parkington Hall

the appearance of his master. When the Count did return, he found it difficult to explain to Nevasta why the wolf-hounds were always hostile to cats, but tried to console him with the news of how the Hall's head groom was going to be responsible for both Nevasta's safe lodgings and welfare.

Prior to Lord Stocksfield's marriage to the much younger Honourable Sarah Linton-Pope, Fantasia had maintained her small but select court just by the foot of the great carved staircase itself. She had been born and brought up in the Hall, as had her mother, grand-father and great-grandmother and father before her. Even one of the outsized oil canvases of Lord Stocksfield's ancestors, which adorned the walls of the great hall as well as up the staircase itself, depicted one of Fantasia's relatives sitting, puffed up and dignified, on Lord Stocksfield's grandmother's lap. In fact, to an observer, it was difficult to decide who looked the more imperious and aloof, the Stocksfield or the chinchilla Persian.

The cats had perhaps reached their zenith at the Hall when Fantasia's mother had been judged the most perfect chinchilla Persian queen in the North of England and, similar to winning an international beauty competition, her mother had been showered by offers which, if they had been accepted, would have taken her around the world. Instead, the Stocksfields had preferred for her to remain at the Hall and raise a family, sired by another chinchilla Persian aristocrat which had been one of her competitors for the title of best Persian cat in the north.

Fantasia had been the first born in a litter of four, and as soon as her eyes had opened on her tenth day of life, her gaze had settled on her ancestor in the oil portrait. From almost that moment on, she had made up her mind that that was the type of cat she would grow up to be like and that, hopefully, she too would be remembered in a similar fashion, by having a portrait with her included prominently on it, hanging in some conspicuous place in those elegant surroundings. But regrettably, the arrival of Lord Stocksfield's second wife and beloved wolf-hounds had dramatically altered Fantasia's world and lifestyle and, as if in exile from her family 'seat', she had lived the last year out in dignified isolation, in her stable-yard quarters, from what she considered to be a part of her rightful inheritance.

Lord Stocksfield had initially made a gallant attempt to arrive at a satisfactory compromise by trying to have the wolf-hounds confined to the south and east wings of the mansion but, alas, neither Lady Stocksfield nor the wolf-hounds would have any of it. So for Fantasia's ultimate safety the chinchilla Persians had had to withdraw to the stable-yard, and the kindly Lord Stocksfield tried to compensate by ensuring that the cats at least received everything they required, and the chief groom was entrusted with the duty of acting as guardian to them. The only concession that Lady Stocksfield would agree to was that the wolf-hounds were banned from either entering or going into the vicinity of the stable-yard.

Now that Nevasta had been turned away from the Hall and had suffered such a humiliation, he was in no mood to concede defeat for a second time in one day. But when he was challenged by Fantasia and her three henchmen, instead of clawing and scratching his way to an accustomed victory, he spat out his pent up contempt of the wolf-hounds with such a degree of fury that the chinchilla Persians became spellbound at the ferocity of the outburst. On learning about what had just happened at the Hall, Fantasia started to warm to this sturdy tiger-striped intruder. Her body relaxed from its arched posture, the fur on her back no longer stood on end, and her tail lowered to the trail position, whilst her eyes reflected a more compassionate and welcoming glow.

Fantasia welcomed Nevasta as if already he was her comrade in arms. Now in the company of what could well turn out to be a powerful ally who shared her hatred and contempt for the outsized dogs who had usurped her position at the Hall, Fantasia formally invited Nevasta into the room, offering him their full hospitality for the duration of his stay at Parkington.

As these two superior cats divulged some of their respective backgrounds to each other, Fantasia's two chinchilla Persian companions remained as quiet as church mice, taking in every word that was uttered, for their mistress was seldom in the habit of relating parts of her noble family history and recent predicament whilst they were around. Also, they felt   privileged at being able to remain present at the 'council of war' that was now to take place.

Nevasta informed Fantasia that he expected his master, the Count, to remain at the Hall for at least the next ten to fourteen days. During this time, he had sworn to himself to seek revenge on the despicable wolf-hounds, and so redeem his self-respect, as well as the honour of felines in general. Now, having shared such thoughts with Fantasia, his resolution transformed itself into that of a mutually agreed crusade. Fantasia and Nevasta rubbed their foreheads together to pledge the pact that they had made between them and, whilst doing so, a few of Fantasia's sensitive snow-white whiskers brushed Nevasta's, which caused her to blush beneath the smokey-grey fur of her cheeks.

Chapter Two

'Operation Wolf-Hound'

The following day, Fantasia promised to provide Nevasta with a detailed plan of the Hall, so that a line of attack on the wolf-hounds could be worked out between them. But, in the meantime, Nevasta expressed an interest in being shown round the stable-yard for, on entering through the impressive wrought-iron gates, in spite of its somewhat ordinary name, it appeared to be quite a stylish environment to inhabit.

The stable-yard stood by itself some quarter of a mile to the north-east of Parkington Hall and was built as a quadrangle in the attractive sandstone of the district. The ornate wrought-iron gates, situated at the south west side of the yard, provided an air of opulence. Water from a small fountain tumbled quietly down into a stout stone drinking trough, which was situated almost in the centre of the flag-stoned yard, and gave a coolness that must have welcomed and refreshed every horse able to take advantage of it. Similarly, it provided a drinking place to a flock of white fantailed pigeons who had their own quarters in a loft on the opposite side of the yard to Fantasia's accommodation. A small clock tower jutted up in the middle of the grey-slated roof of the eastern side of the yard, its gilded Roman numerals contrasting agreeably with the verdigris blemish of its copper hands.

The chief groom's quarters were above the foremost coach house and looked over the yard to the main stables under the clock. It had no windows looking towards the home park, for in those days owners of such properties tried to retain as much privacy as possible. There was a selection of spacious loose-boxes and stalls to comfortably stable well over twenty horses and two mahogany panelled harness rooms boasted some of the best saddlery to be seen in England.

Above some of the stabling were the hay lofts, and it was in these lofts that Fantasia and her companions had their sport with both mice and rats. It was only when involving herself in this type of hunting that she was able to take her mind off those ill-mannered wolf-hounds who had usurped her position at the Hall. How often she had dreamt, when making a successful pounce and pinning one of the rodents down, that she had trapped a wolf-hound with a similar amount of efficiency. But now that Nevasta was her ally, perhaps something equally as effective could materialise.

Nevasta was well pleased with the detailed plan of the Hall which Fantasia had drawn up for him, and he already felt that he knew his way around both the ground and first floors. However, although he was not interested in the cellars, he did require some further information about the attics; so the rest of that day was spent with the help of Fantasia, familiarising himself with the Hall's geography.

As far as all reports signified, the wolf-hounds had really

taken over Fantasia's kingdom lock, stock and barrel. For they were reputed to spend the majority of their leisure hours sprawled out like bear rugs at the foot of the great staircase, in exactly the same place where Fantasia's family used to reside and, of course, the very spot where Fantasia had been born. At the present time, there were four wolf-hounds living at the Hall and when they were not sprawled out in the luxury of their surroundings, they would amble around the majority of the mansion as a part of their daily inspection. Their shaggy muscular bodies always kept together like hounds in a pack, with their heads held high, their long tails swept upwards as if in contempt of anything or anybody that came beneath their towering forms. But perhaps the most foreboding thing about these, the tallest of dog breeds, was how extremely powerful looking their massive grey bodies appeared, and how suicidal it would be for any cat to come within grabbing distance of their guillotine-like smiling jaws. So, after weighing up all the pros and cons, it was quite clear to Nevasta that any sort of physical combat with the wolf-hounds was not worth considering, and that their revenge would have to rely on a more cunning approach. However, whatever was going to be the case, Nevasta insisted on undertaking a preliminary recce of the Hall, so that he could gain a first-hand insight as to its geography, in order to establish the type of revenge that could be masterminded against the vindictive wolf-hounds.

Fantasia thought hard as to how this could be made possible, then she decided that, with her two companions, they could act as decoys and lure the wolf-hounds away from the Hall in the direction of the small summer house and, at the same time, try to get the wolf-hounds into trouble there. If this escapade proved to be successful, Nevasta would have sufficient time to enter the mansion by way of the dairy larder at the north end of the Hall and, providing that all four wolf-hounds took up the chase after the decoys, he should have sufficient time to carry out the required investigation.

This recce part of the operation was put into effect sooner than was at first thought possible, for Fantasia learnt through her network of informers that the carriage had been ordered for 9 a.m. the following day. The Stocksfields had arranged to take the Count on a day's tour of the local countryside, so this proposed absence could only favour Nevasta's chances of success. Ten minutes after nine the following morning, the carriage with the Stocksfields and the Count on board swung gracefully away from Parkington Hall, through the home park along the mile long southern drive. Twenty minutes later, Fantasia and her two companions discreetly stalked a trio of his lordship's semi-domesticated peafowl, flushing them skilfully out of their home environment of a small copse surrounded by iron railings and guided them gently towards the yawning open door of the thatched summer house. When Fantasia considered that it would be impossible for the peafowl to turn back, she gave the signal and the three of them simultaneously sprang at the unsuspecting birds, which caused the two mottled brown peahens to rocket almost vertically, and the spectacular peacock to start a noisy, laborious flapping. But in all cases it was too late, and the birds found themselves within the confines of the summer house. Fantasia was quick to push close the door behind them, although when doing so momentarily trapped the end of the cockbird's ocellated or 'eyed' tail-feathers which, as a consequence, gave the signal for pandemonium to break loose.

The whole area resounded with the loud, ugly, screaming 'may-awe' 'may-awe' call of the peacock, who had never before been so insulted in all of his majestic life, whilst his hens lost their nerves completely and flapped about the place, colliding with one obstacle after another and breaking one of the ornaments on a window-ledge. The baying of the wolf-hounds in full cry was soon audible above the hullabaloo of the summer house, and it was then that Fantasia considered that it was time for her and her companions to beat a hasty retreat to the safety of the nearby copse.

When Nevasta had heard the bays of the wolf-hounds fading away to the south, he entered the hall through the dairy larder window on the north side as planned. Just as Fantasia had told him, he had found the larder door ajar into the passage and, whilst the coast was clear, he was quick to dash noiselessly along the service passage, past the sculleries and the kitchens until he reached the end of the flag-stoned corridor. He then turned left into the carpeted regions of the mansion and, keeping well to the wall, he skirted the main dining room, which took him past the open door of the book-lined walls of the library, then on to the great hall coming immediately opposite to the main front door, through which he had so recently to flee for his life.

Nevasta became extra cautious here, for he knew it was just around the corner to the right that the wolf-hounds had their lair, and where the main staircase started its ascent to the first floor. His dark form slunk silently along the lush carpeted floor, keeping close to the marble-slabbed skirting of the portrait-bedecked walls, until he was forced to come out of the shadows and into full view of the great, ornately-carved oak staircase itself. Here, his nose twitched in protest at the strong pungent smell of hounds and, in spite of the loftiness of the hall, the odour hung like an oppressive cloud of smog over everything. As there was no evidence of the wolf-hounds being present, Nevasta relaxed sufficiently to notice, out of the corner of one eye, the oil painting that included one of Fantasia's illustrious relatives; it certainly looked a remarkably beautiful and aristocratic ancestor.

With the coast clear, Nevasta broke cover and dashed across this part of the hall and straight up the first flight of wide stairs. At this half way point, he paused a while in order to thoroughly take in his surroundings. He curled his body, weaving in and out of the carved banisters, looking down to the left where the wolf-hounds normally sprawled. On the wall opposite him at the corner of the stairs was an arched alcove, which was almost totally occupied by a vast nineteenth century Wedgwood pottery vase, which had spilling out of it an almost equally large tropical fern. Nevasta was quick to realise the potential of such a sizeable breakable ornament, which appeared even now to balance somewhat precariously on the edge of the recess. Nevasta took a closer look at the alcove and found that, due to the gilded vase tapering at the bottom, there was sufficient room for at least two, if not three, cats to get on the ledge behind it.

Nevasta was suddenly startled by a door opening and then closing somewhere downstairs but, as the footsteps went away towards the kitchens, there was no need for further alarm. However, he decided to take no unnecessary chances and quickly sped up the next flight of stairs to the Persian rugs of the first floor. How very different it all was from his master's mansion on the Cote d'Azur. There was no ornate mosaic work here nor oriental tapestries hanging from the walls; it all seemed very uncluttered in comparison. Nevasta followed Fantasia's plan by memory, turning left into a side passage, following this to the end and then turning to the right. Almost at the end of this next corridor there was a small door on the left which was ajar. On the other side of the mahogany-coloured door there was a steep flight of narrow wooden stairs which gave access to some of the servants' bedrooms as well as to a part of the Hall's attics.

Within minutes, Nevasta had found his way into the attics and arrived beneath what he had come in search of - two sizeable reservoir-like water storage tanks - and, sure enough, just as Fantasia had informed him, a small skylight within the eaves was situated just above the smaller of the two tanks. By leaping onto and standing on the partially covered-in section of the top of the tank, with his back wedged against the skylight and his paws firmly pressed against the tank's top, he flexed his body and the skylight moved upwards and open. He made sure that it would not fall closed again by ensuring that the flat metal lever attached to the bottom of the skylight window fell into place onto the notch on the frame used for such a purpose.

Having made sure of his route of escape, he took one more look at the larger of the two water tanks, for the next time he planned to enter this attic it would be dark and, although his eyesight would be well above that of any human or canine in the dark, the better he knew the exact location of the two tanks, the more likely the plan that he was hatching in his bandit-like mind would be to succeed. After a further tour of inspection, he returned to the top of the smaller tank and squeezed his way through the skylight window and onto the grey tile expanse of the massive pitched roofs of Parkington Hall.

Nevasta took a careful note of the route he took over the roofs and along the gullies on his journey to the north end of the mansion, for Fantasia had been careful to impress on him that this was one aspect of the Hall's geography about which she had no first-hand knowledge. When reaching a large lead guttering and catchment area at the top of a down-pipe, Nevasta followed the more gradual fall of the roof levels until he reached a lean-to outbuilding from which he was able to jump onto the top of a mountainous stack of Newcastle coal. From there he scrambled to the ground and, like the prize-fighter athlete that he was, bounded like a tiger to the sanctuary of the stable-yard where Fantasia and her remarkably smug-looking companions were awaiting his safe return, and to inform him as to the outcome of their successful mission.

The last Fantasia had learnt about the goings on both in and about the summer house, was that one of the wolf-hounds, in its effort to get a better look at the pandemonium within, had jumped at one of the windows and put one of his paws through it. The wolf-hound had cut himself in the process, which caused him to howl even more than before. As the volume of the bays had increased, the peafowl became more hysterical and panic-stricken and, prior to Fantasia having completely withdrawn from the area, she had seen the head butler, a valet and one of the gardeners running concernedly in the direction of the hullabaloo.

It was quite late that evening when the cats finally heard, from eavesdropping on the head groom telling his wife, as to what Lord and Lady Stocksfield considered had occurred during their absence from the Hall. Lady Stocksfield had noticed that one of her beloved wolf-hounds was limping slightly and, on inspecting the hound's paw, had seen that it had cut itself quite badly. It was then that the butler had told the Stocksfields how the wolf-hounds must have chased the peafowl into the summer house and had petrified the birds by baying incessantly at them, even breaking a window in their attempt to get in to them.

The head butler had never particularly liked the wolf-hounds and, if he was to be perfectly honest, was quite frightened of them, so the summer house incident had provided him with an ideal opportunity to get them into as much trouble as possible for such apparently bad behaviour. He had gone on to condemn the hounds' characters further by relating that it had been most difficult for him and the valet to call the hounds off and tempt them back to the Hall, for he had been growled and even snarled at by them. Dramatising further, he related how he had returned to the summer house to release the peafowl, only to find the birds almost in a state of total collapse from their ordeal. When he had opened the door, they could only just manage to muster up sufficient energy to stagger out, somewhat drunkenly, back to their refuge of the thick vegetation of the nearby copse.

Lady Stansfield just could not understand what had come over the wolf-hounds and for them to act so irresponsibly. His lordship was as understanding as possible whereas the Count, although keeping his feelings very much to himself, was delighted at this turn of events for, after the hounds' treatment of Nevasta, he had taken an instant dislike to them.

The next ten days Fantasia enjoyed more than any other similar period of time since she had had to be a refugee from the Hall; for she had the opportunity to show Nevasta around many parts of the thousand or so acres of the Parkington Hall estate. The cats utilised the hay loft as a sports stadium, challenging one another with the zeal of Olympic competitors as to which one of them could succeed in catching the most rats and mice. They had two field days stalking and chasing the rabbits in the old warren situated not far from the north lodge, as well as flushing numerous pheasants from the main copse in the home park. However, although Lord Stansfield's prized fantail pigeons were not on their list of permissible prey, they cheekily explored the large circular stone pigeon loft, and were delighted with the way the pigeons reacted to their presence in their midst, by colliding with one another in their anxiety to fly out of the numerous holes high up in the sandstone southern wall of the loft.

They even spent an early morning in the small stone-built boat house on the north side of the lake, situated in the home park to the south of the Hall, and it was here that Fantasia was able to demonstrate to Nevasta the art of catching young perch for breakfast. She had crouched motionlessly on the side of the small, duck-boarded landing stage and, when a sizeable minnow (fry) had swum slowly to feed nearby, she had moved so quickly in scooping the fish out of the water with her paw that two mallard ducks, who had been quietly paddling by the mouth of the boat house, launched themselves into the air squawking their protests at being startled in such a way. Nevasta had been particularly impressed by the professionalism of Fantasia's lightning scoop, which had been similar to a poacher's ability to catch fish by tickling their undersides, and recognised that this was one talent that he had yet to accomplish.

Unfortunately, like all very enjoyable times, the period of fun had to come to an end some time, and this had been realised when Nevasta had learnt that his departure with the Count from Parkington Hall would soon be occurring. It was therefore decided that further retribution on the wolf-hounds had to take place in the very near future and, in order to ensure this, the following night was chosen to put into play their carefully worked out master-plan of 'Operation Wolf-Hound'.

The plans were quite straightforward and, now that the

time had been set to execute their 'Coup de Grace', the excitement and tension grew and the hours could not pass fast enough prior to the launching of their commando-style mission.

The following night, just after the stable-yard clock had solemnly struck midnight, Nevasta and Fantasia, along with her two companions, quietly squeezed through the yard's wrought-iron gates, and stalked off in the direction of the north of the Hall. Just before reaching the stack of coal piled against the small outhouse, they stopped to scoop away the leaves that covered the bean-bag, which they had previously discovered by one of the dustbins and decided to use it as part of their ammunition against the wolf-hounds. They had taken the precaution of carrying the bean-bag and hiding it close to the Hall during the previous night, so that, in doing so, they would not waste unnecessarily any of their strength and energy on the night of the commando raid itself.

Through good teamwork, it was not too long before Fantasia's two companions had managed to drag the bean-bag in their teeth to the mound of coal. Then came the most arduous task for Nevasta, to take the bean-bag in his mouth and to negotiate the drain pipe and reach the guttering above. By using all his strength and, although almost dropping it when it became caught in a creeper, he succeeded in this difficult task.

While Nevasta regained his breath and was joined by Fantasia and her companions on the Hall's roof, the stable-yard clock could be heard striking the quarter to the hour of one. Fantasia had been only too happy to concede the leadership of the night operation fully to Nevasta, for she fully recognised that when taking on such foes as the wolf-hounds, if 'Operation Wolf-Hound' was going to succeed, all the cunning, shrewdness and experience of Nevasta's background was very much required.

After Nevasta had gone over, for the final time, the next stage of the operation, Fantasia's aides took over the responsibility of conveying the bean-bag to the skylight above the water tanks. Some twenty minutes later, they arrived at the spacious lead gully between two pitches in the vast expanse of the mansion's roof. Nevasta grabbed the bean-bag in his mouth and scrambled up to the skylight, disappearing into the attic with it. Whilst waiting for his reappearance, a pair of long-eared bats slightly startled the chinchilla Persians by flying over them and casting their ghost-like shadows on the mirror-like surface of the skylight. Fantasia felt that the drumming of her heart would be heard a mile off, such was her apprehension and excitement. Then the signal came from Nevasta for the rest to join him in the attic.

Once above the water storage tanks, the four cats worked like a well-trained commando team, following Nevasta closely almost within his very shadow. The bean-bag's destination was the top of the larger of the two water storage tanks and, by the time they had managed to achieve this objective, the trio of chinchilla Persians were puffing like steam engines through sheer exhaustion. Nevasta, on the other hand, like the born leader he was, managed to rally his team's spirit by reminding them what successful retribution could soon be theirs, provided that they could muster all of their reserves, the importance for them to keep their nerve, to work to the plan they had agreed, and for them to do exactly as he directed.

Before the planned lowering of the bean-bag over the top of the larger tank (so that it could be positioned to drape over either side of the arm which supported the ball-cock valve regulating the water flow to the storage tank) Nevasta allowed the Persians to rest for a few minutes, whilst he went to check that the door at the foot of the wooden stairs had not been closed. The door had remained ajar and he was pleased to see that no lights were showing beneath the bedroom doors of the servants' quarters. He quickly retraced his steps to the attic and directed the lowering of the bean-bag to the required position. As soon as the bags made contact with the metal arm supporting the ball-cock valve, the copper float at the end of the arm sank gently under its weight into the water, whereupon the float-valve opened and water started to stream liberally into the three-quarter filled tank.

Now that the level of the water in the tank was starting to rise, Nevasta considered that they had no more than ten minutes to prepare the execution of the second part of the master plan, which had to be completed before the water began to flow over the top of the tank onto the wooden-planked floor beneath. In order to co-ordinate the timing, so that both parts of the operation coincided, he detailed one of Fantasia's aides to wait by the tank and, as soon as it was about to brim over and starting to flood the floor beneath, to quickly make its way to the top of the staircase to give them the signal.

There was now no turning back, and an air of excitement gripped the three of them as they moved noiselessly in single file to the more luxurious surroundings of Fantasia's former territory. Fantasia's eyes moistened with nostalgia as she came to the corridor leading to the top of the great staircase which was to the right of her, for the whole atmosphere conjured up so many happy memories. But even such memories hastily disappeared when one of the wolf-hounds was heard to move and whimper slightly from the depths of the shadows of the great hall beneath them. All three cats immediately froze, becoming as alert as an antelope being cornered by a lion. For a few precious minutes they remained as motionless as statues but, as no further wolf-hound noises were heard, the coast appeared to be clear and they crept silently, as only felines can, down the first flight of stairs.

On reaching the alcove, Nevasta sprang effortlessly up onto the ledge and squeezed behind the towering porcelain vase. He was soon followed by Fantasia and her companion. By all three of them having their backs braced against the wall of the alcove, with their paws against the slippery surface of the tapering vase, they managed to slowly push and manoeuvre it to the very brink of the ledge. Nevasta then positioned himself so that he had a good view of the top of the first flight of stairs, so that as soon as Fantasia's aide, from the top of the stairs, gave the signal that the water from the tank was starting to overflow, the final part of the mission could be carried out at the expense and to the detriment of the slumbering wolf-hounds beneath.

Shafts of moonlight filtered through the stained glass of the Stockfields' heraldic shields, which formed the centrepiece of the large window looming above the small landing between the first and second flights of stairs to the first floor. Apart from the sound of the wind gusting on the outside of the lead casement of the windows, the great hall was as silent as a monastery. Then, after only a few minutes, which seemed like hours to the trio of cats wedged behind the vase, came the signal from the top of the stairs. Nevasta, Fantasia and her companion again braced their backs against the wall and pushed with all their might. Almost immediately, the ornate pottery vase masterpiece, with its sizeable fern, toppled over the edge of the ledge and crashed down, missing the padding of the carpet, onto the side of the marble stairway. The vase exploded like a land-mine as it tumbled and disintegrated from one stair to the next.

Parkington Hall's normal serene status was immediately transformed into chaos. Four Irish wolf-hounds jumped into the air as if they had all just come into contact with a powerful electric current. Their shaggy grey fur stood on end, whilst their ivory fangs glistened in the dark shadows of the hallway, as they uttered the most eerie, grotesque howls that sent shivers up the cats' spines. Almost resembling one ball of fluff, the cats disappeared up the second flight of stairs. As they fled, the scent of cats reached the wolf-hounds at the foot of the stairs and they immediately jumped into action and hurled themselves in hot pursuit.

Nevasta's orders to Fantasia and her aides had been explicit. They were to get out of the Hall by way of the skylight as fast as their legs could carry them, whilst he would remain for a time in order to ensure that at least one of the wolf-hounds followed him up to the attic. By the time the largest of the four hounds had made the top of the stairs, Lord Stocksfield, dressed in his nightgown and tassled hat, had emerged from his bedroom which led onto the passage from the right. A second wolf-hound caught up with his leader, who had just spotted Nevasta. In their keenness to reach him, they knocked into his lordship, almost bowling him over as they sped in hot pursuit of Nevasta. Lord Stocksfield had not seen the Count's top cat, but he did see two of the wolf-hounds disappear at the end of the passage in front of him. Then, on looking half way down the stairs, he saw the other two hounds leaping up at the ledge, which until so recently had supported one of his most precious family heirlooms. Due to the concentration of cat scent on the ledge, the two hounds thought that they had homed in on where the cats must surely be, and their baying reached a previously unattained crescendo; whereas his lordship, on seeing some of the broken remains of his priceless vase, could only conclude that the wolf-hounds had just knocked it off the alcove where it had safely been for the last 100 years or so.

Bedlam reigned further when his lordship pulled the trigger of a twelve-bore shotgun that he had gathered up from a corner cupboard on the landing. This event coincided with droplets of water forming on the ornate plaster friezework of the ceiling above him. This pandemonium was added to when Lady Stocksfield, believing that one of her beloved wolf-hounds had been shot by his lordship, screamed in grief. Nevasta's cool nerve and split-second timing had only just saved him from colliding with some of the Hall's servants, as they timidly came out of their rooms in order to go to their master's aid.

Although the leading wolf-hound had almost caught up with Nevasta when he had reached the foot of the carpetless wooden staircase, the small stairs proved to be much easier for a cat to negotiate than they were for the pony-sized wolf-hounds. So Nevasta dashed his way through the shallow stream of water that was now covering the attic's floor, jumped onto the water tank and made his escape through the skylight. By running through the water, Nevasta had copied the cunning of foxes in the way they sometimes manage to shake off the hounds in pursuit of them by taking to shallow water so that their scent can no longer be detected.

Due to the expanse of water and the height of the wolf-hounds' heads, the only cat scent that they were eventually able to gain was the amount on top of the larger of the two water storage tanks. So up the two wolf-hounds tried to jump, but the only thing they succeeded in doing was to dislodge the bean-bag from its position of weighing down the ball-cock valve. The bag sank gracefully to the bottom of the tank, thus erasing any obvious reason for the water tank to overflow in the first place. By the time the head butler arrived on the scene, all he was able to see was two wolf-hounds jumping hysterically up at the storage tank, whilst water still flowed generously down from its sides. When he managed to tempt the two wolf-hounds away from it, the water appeared to stop flowing over the top, so circumstantial evidence, once again, pointed at the wolf-hounds' guilt.

When the first rays of sun started to smile on the stable-yard, the cats' contagious exuberance over what had taken place at the Hall even appeared to have influenced the horses, who seemed to be whinnying to each other far more enthusiastically than usual. For a long time, the wolf-hounds had played games on the horses by startling them as they jumped out, without any prior warning, in front of them. Days at Parkington Hall had undoubtedly been very much more pleasant prior to the wolf-hounds' arrival.

After Lord Stocksfield had completed his thorough investigation of all the facts made available to him about the goings-on in the Hall during the previous night, as well as taking into consideration the summer house episode of just under a fortnight ago, he had come to the conclusion that the wolf-hounds' hereditary hunting instincts were starting to get the better of them, and that their berserk behaviour would have to be curtailed before any further damage was caused to his family heirlooms and inheritance. Although under some degree of protest from Lady Stocksfield, his lordship had insisted that the wolf-hounds' quarters were moved from beneath the great staircase, that they should be confined to a room leading onto a small courtyard situated at the rear of the Hall near the servants' quarters and that, when being exercised in the park by the servants, they must be kept on leads.

Although such measures did not result in the reinstatement

of Fantasia and her companions to their previous position at the Hall, it had contributed a great deal to their feelings of self-respect and a degree of justice and retribution had been realised. However, Fantasia fully recognised that it had all been very much thanks to Nevasta's ingenuity that her revenge on the wolf-hounds had been exacted in such a satisfactory fashion. So the happenings and success of the previous fortnight had been beyond her wildest dreams.

Chapter Three

An Invitation Accepted

During the latter part of Nevasta's stay at Parkington, it had become obvious to Fantasia's companions that a deep-rooted friendship had developed between the blue-blooded chinchilla Persian pedigree, Fantasia, and the tiger-striped ginger, ex-alley cat, Nevasta. Although the cats concerned would undoubtedly have denied that any mutual admiration society existed between them, nevertheless they both admitted to themselves, and only to themselves, that their lives seemed empty and unsettled when they were not in each other's company. Even the Count had observed a change in the behaviour of his 'top cat'. for he had never seen Nevasta pay so much attention to another, as he was now doing to his friend's magnificently furred pedigree, Fantasia.

The Count had invited the Stocksfields to visit his mansion that same summer, but the young Lady Stocksfield had graciously declined the offer, telling the Count that the humid heat of the Cote d'Azur had never agreed with her and, as a result of this, she preferred to remain in the cooler climate of northern England. However, she was anxious not to stand in the way of her husband and prevent him from spending a holiday in the sun with his old university friend, so she went out of her way to encourage Lord Stocksfield to accept the Count's invitation. Also, on a personal note, her ladyship found that she had little in common with the Count and certainly did not want to stay at a house, no matter how fine, with the legendary population of waif and stray cats, for cats had never been her favourite beasts. In Lord Stocksfield's absence, she would be able to pursue her favourite hobbies of riding and painting, and even have her beloved wolf-hounds constantly at her side.

The Count had always boasted about his ability to understand the majority of the sentiments expressed by members of the cat family and, as he wished to satisfy some of his own curiosity to see just how his cat kingdom in the Cote d'Azur would react to having such a blue-blooded feline aristocrat as Fantasia within their midst, he persuaded Lord Stocksfield that, as he would be travelling by himself, he should bring Fantasia with him.

Nevasta and Fantasia received the unexpected news, that their imminent separation would not be for ever, with considerable satisfaction. Nevasta, being the typical Latin, showed his emotion spontaneously by rubbing his forehead and nose against the silky fur of Fantasia's cheek and forehead. Although Fantasia had inherited some of the reserve and inhibitions of the British nobility, she did show a degree of her deep-rooted pleasure at the good tidings by not moving away from Nevasta's attention, and then allowing her well-furred tail to become momentarily entwined with that of her undoubted admirer.

Some three months later, Lord Stocksfield and Fantasia boarded the steam mail-boat at Dover for Calais, after having travelled by rail in first class compartments from Durham to

Dover via London and Canterbury. After embarkation, Fantasia had not particularly enjoyed the smell, nor indeed the movement, of the ferry boat, even whilst it was still moored in the harbour under the lee of the famous white cliffs of Dover. However, some of these initial misgivings were soon shelved when she was taken into the luxurious surroundings of a mahogany-panelled first-class cabin which Lord Stocksfield had reserved for the channel crossing. After a feast of Dover sole, which had been brought to her by an admiring steward, Fantasia settled down to snooze on a comfortable crimson velvet covered dressing table stool, where her thoughts soon melted into dreams: the night when Nevasta and she had avenged the wolf-hounds; the happy days which they had spent together at Parkington Hall; and the great differences between their family backgrounds and pedigrees. Somehow, her association with Nevasta had had some undercurrent about it which she found hard to either define or understand. Her dreaming went on to bridge the gulfs from the past and the present into the future and transposed Fantasia momentarily into the unknowns of the Cote d'Azur.

It was the compressed-air hissings of the donkey-engine on the bow of the ship, hauling in the mooring ropes, that aroused Fantasia from her slumbers and, although she could not remember the exact details of what she was dreaming about at the time of her awakening, she had been pleased to have been snatched out of a rather hazardous situation that her dreams had involved her in. The vibrations of the steamship's engines caused the stern to shudder under the exuberance of the propellers then, to Fantasia's alarm, the whistle emitted a piercing shrill farewell to England, and the ship started to butt its way out into the English Channel.

Fantasia was alone in the cabin, for his lordship had been invited to be on the ship's bridge with the captain to watch the shore lights disappear over the horizon and to witness at first hand the intricacies of navigation. The mahogany panelling of the cabin walls appeared to make the movement of the ship more pronounced and Fantasia found herself beginning to feel decidedly upset inside. She left the comfort of her stool and took refuge under the spacious bunk, squeezing herself between one of its low supports and the corner of the cabin itself. From the partial security of such a position, she found it easier to cope with the apparent acrobatic movements of the steamship.

After Lord Stocksfield, who had always prided himself on being an excellent sailor even in the worst of seas, had enjoyed himself dining with the captain, he was shown by the ever-attentive steward back to his cabin. On re-entering his quarters, to his utmost alarm, he found that there was no sign whatever of his prized pedigree Persian. The portholes were clamped shut and the door had been locked. After concern for Fantasia's welfare had started to erode some of his lordship's normal unruffled self and he was about to retrace his steps to the captain, in order to request him to alert the crew to start a search, Fantasia crawled out from beneath the bunk, looking as dejected as if she had just been rescued from a burning hay loft.

It was not until the following morning after that nightmarish crossing of the English Channel, when Fantasia and her master were half way by train between Calais and Paris, that she began to feel her old self once more. She had breakfasted well, although the milk had seemed far less creamy from what she had been accustomed to. However, the luxurious trappings of the first class compartment on the Calais-Paris express had proved to be most agreeable and she was already getting into the Dick Whittingham mood of an ardent traveller.

On their arrival in Paris, they were met by one of the Count's friends, who had promised the Count that he would meet Lord Stocksfield off the boat train at Gare de Lyon and convey him across Paris to Le Gare du Nord, for his onward journey to the Cote d'Azur. The Count's friend proved to be extremely courteous and, in fact, was good enough to go out of his way to ensure that Lord Stocksfield had an opportunity to see something of Paris before it was time to board the famous Le Train Bleu. As his lordship had not wished to confine Fantasia to a padded travelling box, he had bought for her a smokey-blue coloured collar which sported a small number of expensive looking studs. A long, plaited lead enabled Fantasia to sit comfortably almost where she wished, and already she was absorbing some of the strange smells and foreign characteristics of Paris.

Whilst sitting on the back seat of the Count's friend's De Dion Bouton sports car, Fantasia had caught her first glimpse of a miniature poodle which had been shorn in such a way that the head and shoulders had been left with a lion-like curly mane, whereas the rest of the body had been either completely or partly shorn. Its front legs were clipped up to the elbow, apart from a thick band of frizzy fur left at the knees. Its shorn back legs looked even funnier, for these had not only thick bands of fur left around the knees but, further up the legs, just before the lower thigh, there were more shorn garters of fur. A further ring of nakedness encircled the poodle's back and, to crown what Fantasia considered to be the humility that the poodle had had to suffer for the eccentricity of its owner, a pink silken bow had been tied firmly to the frizzy fetlock of fur which had been left on the crown of its head.

Fantasia realised that this dandified poodle was by no

means the fault of the dog concerned, but rather of some exotic taste of its owner that would turn this member of a courageous working breed into the laughing stock of any self-respecting British canine. Its shorn tail looked as if it had a powder-puff attached to it. What an awful situation it would be for Fantasia if the French custom for dogs was to be adopted for cats, but her mind was soon put at rest when she saw a completely normally attired cat sitting quietly next to a street stall.

The wide, tree-straddled boulevards, restaurant tables plumed with sizeable parasols spilling out over the spacious pavements but shaded by the plane trees, the constant hooting of car horns, and the excitable shoutings of passers-by all seemed to Fantasia to be a very different world and a far cry from the tranquil surroundings of Parkington Hall.

At Maxim's, the Count's friend lunched Lord Stocksfield with all the style and ceremony that was called for when such excellent cuisine was so abundant and his lordship, being the perfect master that he was, ensured that Fantasia had an opportunity to share in some of the fayre. So, after a fine meal of pate de canard a l'orange, followed by venison in port wine with redcurrant jelly, Fantasia suffered some discomfort when she was picked up by her master and carried across the crowded promenade to the De Dion Bouton, parked conspicuously in the graceful surroundings of Le Place de Madeline. The normally horizontal pupils of Fantasia's eyes had become more oval, resembling egg-yolks floating in two sleepy pools of egg-white and it was only then that she realised that the generous helping of venison she had eaten must have been cooked in port wine, and it was now beginning to make an impression on her. Instead of sitting as regally as possible after such an occasion, she could not help but sprawl, in a somewhat intoxicated fashion, over the comfortable leather-upholstered back seat of the automobile and, purring with contentment, she fell into a deep sleep.

At Le Gare du Nord, Lord Stocksfield bade the Count's friend farewell, thanking him warmly for the excellent time that they had spent in his company. His lordship's reserved compartment was located and, some twenty minutes later, Le Train Bleu discharged a blast of steam which caused Fantasia to jump in alarm, the fur on her back standing on end, her whiskers bristling, her needle-like claws sinking deeply into the velvet-covered cushion provided for her use. The iron monster of a steam train flexed its muscles whilst it gathered up its full strength to haul its load of coaches from Le Gare du Nord through the night southwards amidst the vineyards of central France to the history-packed shores of the Mediterranean and the Cote d'Azur. Lord Stocksfield retired to his bed early, for he was not used to consuming so much good food and wine at mid-day. Fantasia lay comfortably on her cushion on the bed adjacent to her master and, with the 'rat-a-tat-tat', 'rat-a-tat-tat' melodies of the coaches' wheels passing over the wooden sleepers, her charcoal-tinted eyelids soon fell gently over her emerald-coloured eyes. Dijon, Lyon, Avignon, and on to the great maritime port of Marseilles which, like a large octopus, sprawled its ungainly form over the coastline, besmearing the intense blue of the sea with patches of grey and brown.

Whilst the train rested at Marseilles, a bowl of the rather strange smelling French milk and a leg of chicken - the latter Fantasia felt must have been dragged through a herb garden, for it was so highly seasoned - were brought to her in the compartment by a tubby steward who exuded 'bonhomie' but, whilst doing so, overwhelmed all those in his immediate vicinity with the nose-twitching smell of garlic. This had been Fantasia's first exposure to the clinging, pungent odour of this bulbous-rooted plant and she had immediately become allergic to it, which caused her to sneeze incessantly. It was only by pressing the inside of her right front paw against her nostrils and breathing through her mouth that she found she could bring her sneezing to an end. Lord Stocksfield had had the window of his compartment opened and, with the influx of fresh air, Fantasia soon recovered her outward composure. While slowly lapping the ivory-coloured milk, she contemplated what other future hazards this foreign country would hold in store for her.

Le Train Bleu seemed to pull its load thankfully away from Marseilles, whilst its enthusiasm for more stylish surroundings appeared to be contagious to all who rode in her. The early morning heat haze was dissolving as a result of the sun climbing its way into the sky in the south-east whilst, in the distance to the north, smokey-blue clouds hovered in clusters above the ridges of the Alpes Maritimes. Already, Fantasia had begun to feel the humidity of the Cote d'Azur, and rather wished that she had the ability to adjust the thickness of her chinchilla-coloured fur when she wanted to. Humans were so lucky in this respect, for they could so easily put on or take off things, all depending on the temperature of their surroundings and just how they felt.

By-passing St. Tropez, the train continued its journey eastwards, making its next major stop at Cannes. Here, Fantasia recognised exactly how adaptable to its surroundings Le Train Bleu was, for its somewhat sombre appearance at Le Gare du Nord had now given way to that of a softer countenance, similar to that adopted by the majority of sun worshippers when their reached their Mecca of the Cote d'Azur. On the latter part of its journey, the railway line clung closer to the coast and, after Nice, plunged with cavalier abandon through hewn-out tunnels in the towering cliffs, passing over bridges spanning deep ravines. In so many places the train, hovering as it was over pyramids of jagged rock caressed by the deep blue sea of the Mediterranean, appeared to Fantasia to be gambling with the laws of gravity, so she felt no regret that the journey had almost come to an end when they arrived at the opulent but elegant station at Monte Carlo.

Whilst Lord Stocksfield had gone out of the compartment, no doubt to ask a steward to help arrange porters for his luggage at their destination, Fantasia checked herself over in the wall mirror, for she had to look her best and be as impeccable as possible for her meeting with Nevasta and her introduction to both the Count's and Nevasta's kingdom of waif and stray alley cats. One thing that she had never forgotten her mother telling her was that first impressions were the ones that counted the most.

With her self-grooming, she repeatedly licked the side of her right paw and started to smooth some of her more rebellious tufts of silken fur under her ears. The dozen or so snow-white, as well as partially black, coarse whiskers arranged as they were in three main rows either side of her muzzle, also needed attention and, with her paw working with great dexterity, she was able to make these whiskers stand out more impressively. The small, ladder-like arrangement of darker whiskers which climbed horizontally above either side of her now terracotta-blemished nose, had become quite unruly so, with the skill of a professional coiffeuse, she brushed the whiskers upwards with the back of her paw, and then patted them gently from side to side to offset them in the most effective fashion. Before finishing her grooming, she wiped over the back of her ears so that they glistened as if they had been freshly shampooed.

Whenever she entered a strange new environment and had to meet others for the first time, Fantasia was aware the she was inclined to adopt an air of aloofness, which often gave those she met a very wrong impression as to her true warm nature. But, no matter how hard she had tried to stop herself assuming such a regal look of disdain, she found that whenever she was either consciously or subconsciously feeling a little nervous, she would hide behind her pedigree family's characteristic of putting on such airs and graces of assumed grandeur; which somehow or other always seemed to boost her flagging confidence.

Just prior to the train completing its strikingly picturesque journey from Monte Carlo to Menton, Lord Stocksfield re-entered the compartment and Fantasia could see immediately that her master had attended to his own appearance with a similar degree of fastidiousness. His lordship stroked Fantasia gently on the side of her neck and she purred her response to this telepathic reassurance from her master, who must have been well aware of her trepidation and concern for her near at hand meeting with Nevasta, and her confrontation with the one hundred and twenty or so waifs and strays of the Count's cat kingdom.

Chapter Four

Chateau Santa Sophia

The Count, the Count's nephew and Nevasta were all on the shaded platform at Menton to welcome Le Train Bleu carrying, as it did, their guests. In spite of the heat of the day, the Count and his nephew were wearing three-piece suits with silken cravats, grey toppers and carrying matching grey gloves. Fantasia immediately recognised the black ebony cane which the Count was carrying, which had his family coat of arms engraved upon its silver top. She had been particularly impressed with this as half of the crest was occupied by two heraldic cats rampant upon it.

When Fantasia was carried from the train by his lordship she saw that Nevasta was being led on a lead by the Count's nephew and looked rather withdrawn and ill at ease, not at all as he had been during his time with her at Parkington Hall. This was, no doubt, due to him having been attached to a lead and the somewhat formal setting of the welcoming ceremony, for their hosts were lined up on the platform to welcome them in a similar fashion as if they had been meeting a Head of State. After greeting his old university friend and introducing him to his nephew Alexandre, the Count patted Fantasia on the dome of her silken head and reminded his nephew of how he had told all his neighbours in the region that their feline guest was the most magnificent-looking cat to ever set foot on the Cote d'Azur. To Fantasia's relief and gratification, Alexandre enthusiastically agreed with his uncle's flattering appraisal of her.

Out of the corner of her eye, Fantasia could see that Nevasta was becoming even more unsettled, twitching the rose-pink triangle of his nose and flicking the end of his ginger-grey-ringed tail. Fantasia imagined that this impatience was due to Nevasta disliking any type of ceremony when he was not playing the leading role. Just as Fantasia was beginning to relax fully, she almost jumped out of Lord Stansfield's arms when the shrill whistle of Le Train Bleu announced its departure from Menton to the Italian border. She wondered why ships and trains could not depart to their respective destinations in a less startling and more relaxed fashion.

Fantasia managed to regain her composure by the time the small party, led by the Count, made its way through the station to his much-loved 3-litre Bentley, which stood outside the station's main entrance. A liveried chauffeur touched the peak of his hat and opened one of the highly polished passenger doors with the Count's heraldic crest with its leopard-like cats emblazoned upon it. Lord Stocksfield's sizeable leather-clad trunks were manhandled on to the top of a back-up vehicle, into which Alexandre climbed with two of his uncle's valets. Fantasia and Nevasta were placed on the bucket seats with their backs to the chauffeur and the glass partition dividing the driver from his passengers and they sat facing their respective masters. Nevasta's mood of uneasiness had begun to make

Fantasia feel unsettled too and it was not until the Bentley had freed itself from the bustle of activities near to the station, and its 3-litre engine had roared into life, that the two cats started to relax in each other's company.

The made-up road soon gave way to the much softer surface of a minor, lesser used highway. Blue gum trees, fifty to sixty feet high, flanked the route on either side, their grey peeling bark and elongated leaves absorbing the sun whilst their presence filled the air with the warm, intoxicating aroma of eucalyptus. After passing several impressive gateways and lodges, the Bentley slowed its pace and, on turning to the right, passed through two of the largest gate columns Fantasia had ever seen. They had arrived at the Count's mansion and Nevasta's adopted home, the Chateau Santa Sophia.

The Bentley came to a standstill outside the heavily studded front door of the chateau, which immediately opened and out came the Count's elderly butler, a number of valets and the housekeeper. All the menfolk were dressed in a similar livery to that of the chauffeur, their silver buttons embossed with the now familiar feline coat of arms. The Count and Lord Stocksfield alighted from the Bentley, followed closely by their two cats, whom they had releaved of their collars and leads. Fantasia felt that the majority of the servants were now gazing most inquisitively at her, as opposed to keeping their eyes on their master. She also had the sensation that she was under surveillance by a galaxy of eyes from the shadows of the vast shrubbery opposite the front doors, and also from behind the dark green foliage and the upright branching of the evergreen Italian cypresses, which seemed to be arranged in regimented columns leading away from either side. In addition to this great attention, through the hall windows, she sensed that there were many more eyes peeping at her from behind the drapes of the heavy velvet curtains within the chateau. One hundred and twenty or so previously homeless cats were in residence, yet not one of them, at this stage, had come out in the open to meet and welcome her.

Lord Stocksfield bent to scratch Fantasia affectionately under her chin and then left her to be taken care of by Nevasta, for the Count had previously informed his friend that there was absolutely nothing to fear, as far as Fantasia was concerned, whilst she was their guest at the Chateau Santa Sophia; for this was a cat's paradise and refuge and, with Nevasta to look after her, nothing could possibly go wrong. As soon as their respective masters and Alexandre had gone inside, Fantasia witnessed the arrival of what appeared to be an increasingly large crowd of the most incredibly marked cats of every shape and size, approaching from all three sides. As the majority of Nevasta's cat kingdom drew closer, the immediate surrounding of the gravel driveway looked as if it was covered with an oriental carpet interwoven with every shade of colour imaginable, so great was the diversity of coats of blacks, browns, gingers, silvers, tortoise-shells, and tabbies with every variety of markings possible.

Once most of the cats had assembled in the driveway in front of the chateau, encircling Nevasta and Fantasia with the same degree of enthusiasm and curiosity with which pop fans surround their idols, Nevasta called them to order. Firstly, with the presence and command of a general addressing his troops, he introduced Fantasia to his subjects of waifs and strays. He reminded all of them that Fantasia was their first guest from the far away kingdom of Great Britain and that, when he had visited her home with their master earlier on that year, he had received the warmest hospitality ever - he graciously omitted to make reference to Lady Stocksfield's cat-hating Irish wolf-hounds at Parkington Hall. In order to repay such hospitality, he requested all present to help make Fantasia's stay at the Chateau Santa Sophia as enjoyable and as memorable as possible.

On the whole, Fantasia felt a great deal of warmth and goodwill generated by the cats around her although, due to her ultra-sensitive nature, she could not help feeling a degree of animosity coming from a small group of sizeable tortoise-shell cats sitting and standing to the rear of Nevasta. One cat, by the name of Fleur, who had pressed forward and managed to attract Nevasta's attention, was introduced to Fantasia. Fleur's mother, who claimed to have pedigree Siamese cat blood in her ancestry, had been born in southern England in the fashionable town of Tunbridge Wells and had been brought to Menton by her mistress, the late Countess of Hawkhurst. When the Countess died, Fleur's mother had been cared for by an old family retainer and it was in her small house that Fleur was born. Fleur had never been told what nationality her father was but, as far as she was concerned, she considered herself rather special for after all, she was an English cat and remarkably proud of her British heritage. As Nevasta had wanted a member of his kingdom to attend to Fantasia's needs, due to Fleur's keenness to be connected with this British feline aristocrat, she was appointed to act as her companion throughout her stay.

Nevasta introduced Fantasia to some of the hierarchy of his kingdom, after which he turned towards the open front door of the chateau and, as he did so, his feline subjects melted away as guests attending a palace tea party will do, once the sovereign has departed. By tradition, it was the privilege of only a handful of cats to enter the chateau by its front door. However, on this occasion, instead of some of the chosen few following Nevasta, they too had discreetly withdrawn, for they had previously been informed that Nevasta wished to show Fantasia around the chateau by himself.

As she followed Nevasta through the porch, Fantasia had observed the heraldic cats on the Count's coat of arms seemingly grinning down at her from above the massive arch of the front door. Every time she had come across the Count's family crest, she had felt more reassured. Once past the inner double doors, they entered the chateau's great hall, which could not have been more dissimilar to that of Parkington Hall, for it displayed a degree of extravagant richness of a typically Byzantine period style. Ornamental mosaic work spread like carpets and tapestries over floors, walls and ceilings. Horizontal gilded framed panels boasted silver-leaf backed mirrors, which exaggerated and multiplied both the colours and extent of the lavish peppering of mosaics. In spite of the lack of furniture in the great hall, the whole area appeared to be ablaze with richness. Even the smiling smoothness of the marble pillars boasted a selection of mysteriously intertwined lines of Arabic characters. The only factor that could be compared with that of the hall at Parkington was the large collection of out-sized family portraits, which seemed to cling lovingly to the walls, as they followed the grand staircase upwards to the first floor.

With the curving grand staircase to the left of them, Nevasta led the way across the hall to some double-panelled doors situated at the far end of the hall to the right. They entered the mansion's dining room and, instead of a large wooden dining table, Fantasia saw a table of marble, surrounded by eighteen of the highest-backed carved chairs imaginable. Although the seats had once been extravagantly covered with a rose pink moire silken material, the upholstery showed countless signs of clawing, as did the floor to ceiling curtains, with some of the voile linings extensively torn and lacerated.

Nevasta, on seeing Fantasia's obvious concern as to what could only be the cat residents' treatment of the seats and curtains, explained that when the Count was not entertaining humans he would have feasts for the cats to enjoy. When all the invited cats had overeaten and begun to relax, not surprisingly they would dig their claws into the chairs and then loosen up by playing after-dinner games, vying with each other as to who could climb to the highest point up the backs of the curtains. Even the silken-tasselled bell ropes had not escaped the attention of the cats at play for, apart from the tassels, even the lower part of the ropes themselves had been shredded by the constant flicking of their claws.

Walking past the far end of the marble table, the two cats entered an anteroom just to the west of the dining room which was situated on the north-western corner of the mansion. In the centre of the anteroom was a marble fountain which totally captivated Fantasia's attention for, supporting the large alabaster bowl, were twelve black marble lions. Seeing how Fantasia was intrigued by this, Nevasta went to a floor button switch behind a curtain and, when he had pressed it with both of his front paws, water started to spill from the top of the fountain and also flowed gently from the mouths of a dozen cherubs into the large shallow bowl beneath.

Fantasia followed Nevasta as he sprang up onto the top of a throne-like seat situated in front of one of the tall windows to the western side of the chateau. Looking out of the window she saw, beyond an ornate balustrade beneath them, the land falling away to the azure-blue sea and, across the bay, Monte Carlo. Reverting her gaze into the chateau, she stared in fascination through the tumbling water of the fountain, back into the dining room. Everything now seemed more and more like a dream, but she was soon jolted back into reality when Nevasta jumped effortlessly from the throne-like chair onto the rim of the fountain and started lapping the bubbling water from the large saucer-type alabaster bowl. He walked with all the agility of a trapeze artist around the circumference of the bowl, giving the impression that even the black marble lions supporting it were among his subjects. With a further effortless jump, Nevasta returned to the throne chair and told Fantasia that only he was allowed to drink from the bowl but, as she was an honoured guest, she could share the privilege with him.

Apart from the dining room leading into the anteroom where the fountain was situated, the state room also had access to it on its southern side. Here, the majority of the mosaic work on the floor and the ceiling depicted various different species of tropical birds and one could well imagine the type of sensation this must have presented to any cat which had not previously been exposed to so many appealing birds. The centre pieces of both the marble floor and the painted ceiling were identical circles of six large Indian peacocks with their respective fan-type tails erected in full display. Fantasia looked at Nevasta and they both recalled their first triumph over the wolf-hounds, with the trapping of the Parkington Hall peafowl in the summer house. Within the two circles of peacocks were the four main compass bearings. Four floor to ceiling windows flanked a pair of sizeable French windows which gave access to a small balcony and it was from this that Fantasia had her first, almost interrupted view across the bay of Menton to the principality of Monaco. She felt sure that there could not have been a more dramatic view of Monte Carlo, for even the palace battlements stood out like impregnable suits of armour and the pinks and whites of the buildings contrasted magnificently with the wealth of ink-blue sea.

The doors opposite the French windows opened into the great hall but, before re-entering this, Nevasta led Fantasia from the state room into the smaller drawing room. In this, apart from being dressed with a more delicate pinkish shade of furnishings and mosaics, a large Bechstein concert grand piano stood impressively, just to the front of a cave-like illuminated alcove which boasted an oil mural of St. Francis of Assisi. They paused for a moment in front of the alcove to show their respect to the patron saint of the animal kingdom, with Fantasia closing her eyes for a moment's reflection and, before gathering herself together, sought the saint's counsel and guidance for the duration of her stay at the Chateau Santa Sophia.

Nevasta sensed that he had momentarily lost Fantasia's attention but, although he had never paid much notice to the mural nor to any particular allegiance apart from that which he had to the Count, he had always respected other individuals' particular leanings and values - provided, of course, that these did not conflict with what he required of his subjects. He had also been pleased to see his guest's obvious approval of everything that she had seen for it had been his intention to impress. He led the way out of a small door from the drawing room back into the great hall. They did not cross the great hall to the grand staircase, for one of the Count's liveried footmen opened a small door to the left of them, then pulled back a latticed grille, which gave access to a lift.

Fantasia had never been in a lift before and was slightly nervous when she walked over the threshold. However, she was determined to remain unruffled and not to let Nevasta be aware of her concern. She watched the servant pull the sliding grille to and push a white ivory button embossed with the number three. The box-like lift jolted and Fantasia shuffled backwards until the base of her tail was firmly wedged against the lift's rear wall, whereupon the tip of it developed a nervous twitch. Just as she felt that her stomach had climbed into her mouth, the antiquated lift shuddered to a standstill. Firstly, the sliding grille was pulled to one side, then a door was opened and Fantasia, like a cat leaving a sinking ship, was quick to leave the lift, although she did so with all the dignity that she considered befell such a well brought-up cat of her pedigree.

It was on the third floor of the chateau that they were rejoined by some of Nevasta's senior cats, as well as Fantasia's newly appointed companion, Fleur. Walking down the corridor, almost in procession, Nevasta guided Fantasia into a room which was situated in the chateau's tallest turret and it was from here that Nevasta explained how he controlled his kingdom and administered justice to his subjects, for it was from this room that he held court.

Nevasta had always styled himself as a benevolent feline dictator. He was exceedingly proud of his back street ancestry, and prouder still of the way in which he had worked his way up through the ranks in order to become the Count's trusted top cat. His philosophy was very much based on leading by example, always exerting his authority with firmness but always giving credit to those who were loyal to the kingdom. Nevasta only punished those whom he considered had disobeyed his orders or to have let down the standards to which he had set. The kingdom itself was split into five different sections, numbering some twenty-five cats in each. At the head of each of these was a section leader called a Senator, and under each Senator were three Deputies. The five Senators and fifteen Deputies made up Nevasta's governing body, and all the members of this hierarchy had now assembled to welcome Fantasia officially to their midst.

As she listened to Nevasta's gracious words, as well as to some equally flattering ones from one of the Senators, Fantasia sensed that not all the cats in the room shared the favourable sentiments that had been so eloquently expressed. For she had noticed out of the corner of one of her emotionally-moistened eyes, one of the large tortoise-shelled cats, whom she had observed at the recent assembly in front of the chateau, sitting amongst the Deputies, whose emerald-tinted slit eyes appeared to only signal envy and hatred towards her. Fantasia made a mental note that, once she was alone with Fleur, she must enquire about everything there was to know concerning the evil-looking tortoise-shell female cat.

When the business of the morning was over and Fantasia had thanked all those present for their warmest of welcomes, she was shown by Nevasta to what were to be her quarters during her stay at the chateau. Once Nevasta and two of his aides had withdrawn and disappeared down the marble staircase, Fantasia requested Fleur to tell her everything she knew about the tortoise-shell antagonist. Fleur, similar to a dedicated gossip-column journalist, went over every bit, every crumb of knowledge, gossip and intrigue she could recall about the Deputy cat in question.

The large tortoise-shell female was known as Bethsheba and she had only been at the chateau for two and a half years but, through her ruthless scheming, she had soon risen through the ranks to become a Deputy. Prior to Nevasta accompanying the Count on his trip earlier on that year to Lord Stocksfield in England, she had been seen frequently in Nevasta's company and she had been very much tipped to be Nevasta's future long-term companion. However, on Nevasta's return from England, this hitherto close relationship appeared to have broken down completely and, when rumours began to circulate within the chateau that the most aristocratic cat would soon be paying a visit with the Count's English friend, the cat kingdom had bubbled with curiosity and intrigue. One report had even gone as far as relating that their top cat would take the English pedigree Persian as his future constant companion.

During the weeks leading up to Fantasia's visit, the rank and file of the cat kingdom had observed their leader becoming more dashing and happy, whilst they noticed that Bethsheba was more bad tempered and spiteful. Through her jealousy towards her unknown rival, she had sown the seeds of several unworthy rumours, all centring around the theme that Nevasta was too full of his own importance and beginning to turn his back on his own low-born but respected heritage, only now being interested in blue-blooded feline aristocrats. Of course, nothing could have been further from the truth yet some cats, who bore the odd grudge against Nevasta, were prepared to believe such malicious gossip.

Whilst Fantasia enjoyed an afternoon siesta, laying sprawled over a silken, feather-stuffed bolster, conveniently situated in a pool of sunshine, she mulled over the events since her arrival at the Count's mansion. She had been immensely impressed by most of what she had seen and was very grateful to Nevasta for all the courtesy he had shown her, for he certainly had a wonderful kingdom at the Chateau Santa Sophia. Although she had known previously that Nevasta thought a great deal of her, she had not realised before Fleur's disclosures just how deep his friendship was for her. Of course, she knew just how agreeable she found his company but the question of becoming his permanent companion should surely not be considered, for her parents had always instilled in her that, in the Persian cat world, chinchilla Persians must only become involved with chinchilla Persians. Also, her allegiance was to her aristocratic dynasty and to Lord Stocksfield's family. She reminded herself, too, of her ambition to be portrayed in one of the family portraits that adorned the walls of the grand staircase at Parkington Hall.

Chapter Five

The Abbot's Tomb

The ensuing days were as agreeable to Fantasia as nectar is to a humming-bird; for not only were the grounds of the chateau as impressive as the chateau itself, but also Nevasta had arranged her time in a way which undoubtedly would have done credit to royalty.

To the south of the chateau, one of the avenues of Italian cypresses led to a sunken rose garden which had been arranged in an equally orderly way as had the cypresses. A large, circular lily pond gave relief to the inhospitable thorny stems of the regimented roses, for lily leaves sprawled in a relaxed fashion over the pond's surface, their undersides occasionally being prodded by goldfish and their plate-like tops splashed by the gentle shower from the fountain in their midst. At the south end of the garden was a flight of quite steep, narrow steps and, at the top of these, was an ornate summer house made of stone and panelled with mosaics, which portrayed an Oriental fairy-tale concluding with a dragon devouring a serpent.

When Nevasta had first taken Fantasia up to the summer

house, she had become so unnerved at the sight of one of the very life-like serpents that he had to draw her attention away from it by swiftly ordering an accompanying Deputy to turn on a tap which, when open, allowed water to tumble gently down either side of the flag-stone stairway to the lily pond beneath. Fantasia experienced the sensation of being able to walk down the middle of the steps, with water on either side of her, yet remaining completely dry. How different everything was from Parkington Hall.

The western entrance to the mansion was a copy of a Florentine piazza, built over a hundred and fifty years ago by Italian stonemasons. Falling away from the entrance were some exceedingly wide, shallow steps, at least eight to ten cat-lengths in width, which fell away flight by flight to the inky-blue carpet of the Mediterranean below. The granite stairs were flanked on either side by impressive balustrades, where cats could curl in and out, and these were surmounted by pink marble banisters which appeared to flow like veins from the life-giving sea beneath.

A group of eight red cedars, narrow in girth and very erect in shape, like large evergreen pencils, towered some eighty to ninety feet over the top of the stairway but, between these and the sea were pepperings of the rather conical evergreen pines with their top branches sprawling horizontally. Their straight trunks were reddish-brown, but in places Fantasia had detected that scales of bark had been scratched away, revealing a much redder complexion beneath.

At the foot of this fine array of steps was situated a chapel, built on the site of an old monastery shrouded in legend. The sea lapped gently at the arched foundations of the chapel, which looked as though they were an extension of the rugged rocks beneath. Fantasia had taken an instant dislike to this part of Nevasta's cat kingdom, but had hidden her unease as best she could. The floors of the entrance, and the chapel itself, were decorated with the now familiar mosaics, some depicting palm trees, dates, monks and various species of birds. Cool apricot marble columns supported the small domed roof and a black marble altar standing on a pure white plinth was overlooked by an ancient wooden figure of a little-known saint. Two ornately carved wooden coffins stood solidly on either side of the small aisle.

Fantasia found that the damp and coldness of the dimly lit chapel sent shivers up her spine to such a degree that the hairs on her back began to rise and her tail twitched nervously. Nevasta, as on previous occasions, was quick to sense her discomfort and guided her quickly to a small balcony overlooking the bay. Here, the warm sun-rays obligingly penetrated through the coarser hairs of her outer coat to the silky underfur clothing her body. Fantasia made up her mind then that, if she was going to say a prayer anywhere whilst a guest at Chateau Santa Sophia, it would be in front of the oil mural of St. Francis of Assisi in the chateau, rather than in the eerie setting of this now disused chapel.

The weather during these memorable days was, on the whole, hot and humid - a pleasant contrast to the swirling mists and penetrating drizzle of the north of England, although at times the humidity was a little too much for Fantasia so that her luxurious fur coat lost some of its lustre and became rather bedraggled. However, the almost daily 'mistral' brought refreshing breezes from North Africa and Nevasta told her that it even brought sand from the Sahara Desert to the Cote d'Azur.

Similar to a medieval nobleman and his princes, Nevasta had reserved the sport of hunting lizards and geckos for himself and members of his council of Senators and Deputies. The rank and file could hunt any of the rodent population but on no account could they touch the lizard family, for Nevasta considered that such privileges gave the lower ranks of cats something to strive for, which helped to sort out the future leaders of his kingdom. Sports time usually took place at the warmest part of the day, around noon, for it was at this time that the lizards and geckos were out in their greatest numbers, basking in the penetrating rays of the sun and running in and out and up and down the columns of the balustrades of the flights of granite stairways which descended so graciously to the sea.

Sometimes teams would compete with each other. Two of the five Senators would pick a team of seven each and, as the stairway levelled off in five stages on its way to the sea, each team would take up its position on either side at each stage from top to bottom. Remaining motionless for up to five minutes, to give the reptiles sufficient time to recover from any disturbance and come out once more to bathe in the sun, they would commence the hunt, with each team member sticking to his or her side of the steps and, keeping to the confines of the series of steps concerned, they would try to catch as many lizards and geckos as they could within a period of ten minutes. The team securing the most was the winner, and there was always fierce rivalry between the five sections of Nevasta's kingdom.

The 'eyed' lizard and the wall gecko were the two species most frequently hunted. The slender bodied lizard with the very long tail gained its name because its green body, with a black net-like camouflage over it, was spotted with blue 'eyes'. and the sun bounced off these, giving the effect of a series of miniature volcanoes. The flattened, plump body of the geckos with tubercled feet and flat toes remained motionless to the last second, seemingly stuck to the balustrade at every angle possible. Some of the lizards had parts of their long tails missing - some due to scraps between themselves and some due to managing to make a last minute mistake at a previous cats' sports day. The geckos were seldom so lucky, for they often left their escape too late and the cats would flick them off the columns of the balustrade. The only time the lizards and geckos got the upper hand was when some of their feline predators, in their impatience to catch as many of them as possible in the time allowed, could be lured into a group of wasps, or would become momentarily wedged in some of the narrower gaps between the columns. Also, on some occasions, the cats had been known to try to balance on the pink marble banister and, through its smoothness, fall onto their backs and become bruised. Although Fantasia never joined one of the teams, she did display her agility and style by catching a lizard and a gecko as a result of one pounce. Her sporting activities in the main hayloft in the stable-yard at Parkington Hall had provided her with a great deal of practice in the art of hunting.

Although Nevasta spent most of his day with Fantasia, he also had to keep his eye on the running of his kingdom; so, when he was not with her and Fantasia was not in her quarters with Fleur, one of his Deputies was instructed to chaperone her. However, Lord Stocksfield visited her at least once a day, sometimes coming to her quarters if they had not come across one another either in the chateau or in the grounds. Fantasia sensed that her master appeared to be more at ease in this feline environment and, for a moment, she reflected on her mistress's unsociable and aggressive wolf-hounds which had taken away her rightful place at Parkington Hall.

The only other resident animals at Chateau Santa Sofia were three donkeys and a small spur-thighed tortoise; the latter had suddenly appeared some two years ago, wandering rather aimlessly up the front drive and, as the majority of the cats had never seen a tortoise before, the alarm was raised and the newcomer was soon surrounded by a cauldron of quizzical cats. One tried to pat its naked head but sprang back in fright when it retreated into the safety of its shell. When the cats looked around to see where the head had gone, they were genuinely relieved to see it reappearing slowly from underneath the shell. They called the tortoise Caput, and it had become a firm favourite in the cat kingdom. The donkeys appeared to be anywhere they considered they could get the maximum amount of food with the minimum effort and the chefs of the chateau were constantly chasing them away from the kitchen and stores. The oldest of the three donkeys, known as Knuzo, had been saved by the Count from being ill-treated and overworked in a small hamlet in the hills above Menton. Through good feeding and little exercise, Knuzo had developed a back like a comfortable divan on which he allowed up to two cats to sprawl, for not only did they help to minimise the number of flies around him, but they were also in the habit of scratching his back, an attention that he always enjoyed. Nevasta had taken Fantasia for a ride on Knuzo and Alexandre had recorded the event by taking a photograph of them both for his uncle's family album. Fantasia had been pleased to overhear her master asking Alexandre for a copy of the photograph.

Just about everything concerning the visit had worked out to be as blissful as a dream of life in Utopia: the great variety of fresh fish brought up daily from the Mediterranean, her sumptuous quarters, the warmth and cheerfulness of the smiling sun, the company of so many fascinatingly interesting cats and the general relaxed atmosphere throughout the chateau were as near to paradise as she had ever experienced. However, there were two factors which Fantasia found difficult to understand or control. First, after the second week of her stay, Nevasta had become increasingly attentive and, whenever he left her she felt a strange sense of isolation. Second, Nevasta appeared to be more possessive of her, and her thoughts had become more entangled in a web of fascination for him. Bethsheba, the estranged tortoise-shell cat, had become even more bitter. Fantasia tried to avoid her as much as possible, but this was proving to be increasingly difficult due to the fact that, the more she tried, the more she kept bumping into her. It was almost as though Bethsheba was keeping track of her movements and, when she was not present herself, one of the other large tortoise-shell relations seemed to be glaring at her through their equally mean green saucer-like eyes.

It was late on a Sunday afternoon that Fantasia's life suddenly became engulfed in a nightmare. Nevasta had just left her with Fleur by the summer-house above the rose garden, for the Count had arranged a special banquet for the cats in the marble dining room that evening and Nevasta had to run over the final arrangements for the festivities. Fleur was attracted by a strange noise coming from inside the summer-house and walked in to see what it was, when the door slammed behind her. Fantasia had remained sitting with her powder-puff front paws neatly together, absorbing the tranquillity of the setting, when she felt what appeared to be a blanket draped over her. She struggled to come out from underneath it, but soon realised that she was inside a thick hessian sack. She hissed and spat, spat and hissed, clawing wildly as she did so in an effort to free herself. She then felt the bag being moved and dragged downhill, not bumping down the steps but rather being pulled over the ground, for she could feel the roughness of the stony earth beneath her.

Fantasia felt quite bruised and out of breath when the sack eventually came to a standstill. Then, on hearing the sound of waves breaking over the rocks beneath her, she started to panic. Thinking that she was about to be drowned, she uttered the loudest miaows she could muster, followed by a series of equally highly compressed hisses. She clawed and bit the inside of the sack furiously, fearing that at any moment her end would come, with the sack being allowed to tumble down over the rocks into the depths of the inky blue sea.

Then, as the sack moved, she experienced a smoothness beneath her as it was dragged like quicksilver across a hallway or room floor. She then sensed the dankness of the old chapel. Once more, the sack became stationary and she heard the spine-chilling noise of unoiled door hinges squeaking open. Her sack was then dragged along what must have been a flagstoned passage and, after a pause, she heard what sounded like a large wooden lid being opened, the sack was dragged up the side of a wooden surface, rested on top and then allowed to slither down the other side onto a base. After a further pause, it was bumped down some steep steps and the fustiness of the dank air caused Fantasia to feel suffocated within the confines of the sack. Everything then fell silent and for a time she lay motionless, as if she had been mortally hurt. She then sensed the presence of at least three other cats about her, but after a while no further noise could be heard until, once more, there was the eerie squeaking of the hinges of what must have been a dungeon-type door closing behind the departing kidnappers.

Fantasia continued to remain motionless for a while but, when she realised that she could no longer breathe properly, she made another bid to escape and this time she found that the nape of the sack had been untied and she emerged into a small dungeon of a room, whose only light came through what looked like ventilation holes on either side at the top of the walls. Although she was dazed by her experience and sudden change of fortune, she climbed up the moist steps down which she had recently been bumped, only to find at the top an arched wooden roof about the length and width of one of the two coffins which she had seen during her first visit to the chapel with Nevasta. Try as she might, in no way could she get the top of the coffin to move, for it must have been locked from the outside; so Fantasia, feeling as dejected as any cat could possibly feel, stumbled down the seven steep steps and, in order to keep her paws out of the damp, took up a sitting position on the thick bag which had brought her there.

The more she thought of her present predicament, the more distressed she became. Her eyes started to swim with tears. She sniffed, then shivered, then went through a stage of acute depression but, before her flagging spirits could descend any further into total helplessness, her mind went back to her birthplace by the foot of the great carved staircase at Parkington Hall. Memories of the oil painting of her aloof and dignified ancestor somehow gave her renewed confidence, for her upbringing as a pedigree chinchilla had taught her that, no matter what fate she experienced, she must never let down the high standards of her dignified ancestry and the entire chinchilla Persian dynasty. This sudden flight of mind into the past acted as a total stimulus to Fantasia and, like a patriot suddenly called to defend her country, she shook herself and adopted the mood of a stubborn never-give-in aristocrat in an attempt to live up to how she would have expected her ancestors to behave if subjected to similar circumstances. After a good hour or two of sitting on the bag and receiving no communication from the outside world, as she had become increasingly cold, she decided to creep back into the warmth of the bag, taking the precaution of keeping the triangle of her red brick nose just protruding from the sack's nape and keeping one eye on the steps.

Back at the chateau, Nevasta was beside himself with concern, for he had left Fantasia and Fleur at 4.30 in the afternoon and when, at a quarter to six he had gone to Fantasia's quarters to tell her about the pecking order and procedure at the banquet, there had been no sign of either her or Fleur. On retracing his tracks to where he had last seen them both in the vicinity of the summer-house, he found the equally distressed Fleur trapped within the summer-house itself. In tears, she divulged all she knew about what had happened, which really only conveyed to Nevasta the fact that the door of the summer-house had been shut behind her and from that time she had neither heard from nor seen Fantasia.

Nevasta was quick to rustle up a search party of over twenty cats - some of them to search the rose garden and lily pond, and others the drives, lodges, stableyard and gardens in the vicinity of the chateau. Seven o'clock struck and there was still no sign of Fantasia. Nevasta was now certain that some evil wind had blown over her, for she had never been alone or out like this before. A hasty council of war took place with the majority of the Senators and Deputies present. As the banquet was scheduled to begin at eight, search parties continued to comb the chateau from attics to cellars and from the mansion to the sea but still not the remotest sign of Fantasia was found.

Fantasia imprisoned in the Abbot's Tomb

The Count was told about Fantasia's disappearance and he and Alexandre immediately checked several places. Having no success, the Count broke the news to Lord Stocksfield. His lordship was devastated. Had Fantasia been bitten by a venomous snake? Had she fallen off a rock and drowned in the sea? Had she fallen down the well? Had she got lost on the estate or been shut in a room by mistake?

The Count tried to console his friend by explaining that all these remote possibilities were highly unlikely and he was sure that Fantasia would turn up sometime during the course of the evening. It was therefore decided that the banquet would go ahead as planned.

One of Nevasta's search parties had actually entered the chapel but, on seeing nothing amiss and no signs of Fantasia, had been quick to leave again. Just before eight, the main search had to be called off so that those attending the banquet in the marble dining room could assemble prior to the arrival of the Count and his guests. Lord Stocksfield adopted the typically British 'stiff upper lip', trying not to show how really miserable he was feeling, whereas the Count and Alexandre looked more concerned, for they held themselves very much responsible for Fantasia's disappearance.

Whilst the rank and file of cats that were present ate at random from the extensive hors d'oeuvre, with such delicacies as caviare, sardines, salmon and eel pie, with masses of creamy milk to wash it all down, Fantasia was still trapped in the Abbot's tomb. Daylight no longer filtered through the ventilation holes, and the only noise that she could hear was the sea lapping over the rocks upon which the chapel's foundations were built. Just before darkness fell, she had had another look around the small dungeon, as well as having climbed the steep steps again but, not finding anything that could possibly be regarded as an avenue of escape, she had returned, miserable and cold, to the comparative warmth of the bag. Although she was, by now, feeling hungry, she managed to fall into a shallow sleep and her dreams continued from where they had left off, back in the safe surroundings of the stable-yard at Parkington Hall, enjoying her favourite sport of chasing rat and mouse populations in the various hay lofts and sharing such experiences, not only with her three Persian companions but, some four weeks previously, with her favourite non-Persian companion, Nevasta, too.

Chapter Six

Patachou's Confession

antasia was awakened the following morning just after sunrise, when she heard what sounded like a small quantity of soft fruit falling onto the floor from the ceiling. On leaving the bag, she inspected the items in the dim light of the dungeon and found them to be, not fruit, but a number of fish heads. A selection of eyes from the small pile of heads stared meaninglessly at her and she in turn looked up to the top of the wall above where the fish heads had landed and could just see a small opening like a shaft; so someone who knew about her imprisonment in the tomb must have decided to deliver some food to her, either with or without the kidnappers' knowledge.

Shafts of sunlight entered through some ventilation holes in the wall of the dungeon from the east and Fantasia decided that, if she was to remain fit, she must do as much exercise as possible. The small flight of seven stairs at one end of the dungeon were still as slimy as when she had slithered down them on the previous evening but, as she kept running up and down the middle of the steps, they became drier and not so dangerous. Once she had completed her first bout of exercise, she was sufficiently hungry to tackle some of the fish heads. Although such food would not normally have received a second look from her, she had decided that, if she was going to survive, she must make the best of every opportunity that presented itself, for who knew when the next food would arrive, if ever?

When nightfall fell on the second day, Lord Stocksfield had convinced himself that his aristocrat of cats had met with an accident and had drowned. In all probability, she had gone down to the shore and a wave had washed her off one of the rocks for, after all, the lake in the home park at Parkington Hall never had waves and so Fantasia would be unprepared for such an event. The Count and Alexandre had intensified their search, directing the chateau's servants accordingly, whereas Nevasta had not slept since Fantasia's disappearance having, with a small party of his most trusted friends, been over the entire mansion, looking into every nook and cranny. As no sign of Fantasia was evident, he began to consider that there could be some credence in Lord Stocksfield's belief, although his sixth sense seemed to tell him that his now most treasured companion was still alive. Also, as the Mediterranean was not tidal like a normal sea, if Fantasia had been washed off one of the rocks and drowned, surely her body would have been found.

As the days went by without any hint at all of what had happened to Fantasia, both Nevasta and Lord Stocksfield became more and more despondent. The Count had even had a word with the local chief of police, asking him to investigate the chances of her having been stolen for, as far as he was concerned, she had undoubtedly been the most beautiful cat to ever set foot on the Cote d'Azur. Although the investigation carried out by the police failed to cast any fresh light as to Fantasia's fate, the very thought of someone kidnapping her fired Nevasta's imagination with new avenues of thought. If anyone was going to do such a gruesome thing, they would have to have a motive and, to his mind, a human would only kidnap her for financial gain and, as no ransom note had been received, he ruled that possibility out. Also, the police enquiries had not presented one clue indicating human involvement. Nevasta therefore considered the potential of any of his subjects kidnapping Fantasia in order to get rid of her. However, it was a few days before he received a clue which endorsed one of his lines of thought as to what could have happened to her.

Fortunately for Fantasia, in spite of her general health beginning to deteriorate, the supply of fish heads continued to be delivered daily through the small shaft in the roof. If, just after sunrise, such rations were rather meagre, they would be topped up before dusk. Due to the dankness of the dungeon and the very low light level of her enforced environment, there was a profusion of insect life, spiders in particular. Fantasia had never really taken much notice of spiders before, although there always seemed to have been quite a healthy population of them at Parkington Hall. Now that she was confined to such a small area with nothing to occupy her mind, she had kept watch on one particularly large specimen and was totally fascinated by its hunting activities, for it was a representative of a family that do not make webs to trap their prey, but rather lie patiently in wait and then, with great dexterity, catch and devour it. Most of the spiders were covered in dark brown hairs with patterns of black and white, and seemed to have their own territory, living in aloof tolerance of each other.

Although Fantasia was ensuring that she did as many trips

up and down the seven stairs as she could manage each day, after the fifth day she realised that something must happen quite soon in her favour if her general health was not to sink too low and, as a consequence, she would not see the outside world again. She reflected on the Count's words to her master on their arrival regarding her welfare during this visit, that there was nothing to fear for this was a cat's paradise and refuge. Also, she thought of Nevasta's welcoming speech when he had instructed his subjects to do everything to help make her stay at the chateau as enjoyable and as memorable as possible. Those were happy days.

By the seventh day after Fantasia's disappearance, it was Lord Stocksfield's time to return to England and, if he had thought for one second that there was a possibility that his treasured cat from his ancestral home was still alive, he would have remained. However, he was now reconciled to the conclusion that she had drowned. When the Count bade farewell to his lordship, he told him that he will have a small but choicely designed grey marble plaque made with appropriate wording engraved upon it in memory of Fantasia. And this would be positioned near to the summer-house overlooking the sunken rose garden with its fountain and lily pond, for this was where both Nevasta and Fleur had last seen her alive.

It was Knuzo, the divan-backed donkey, that provided the eventual lead to the true whereabouts of Fantasia. It had been the head chef's practice, on his way back to his own lodgings late at night, to leave a small offering of bread and fish on a ledge just outside the place where the three donkeys usually rested for the night. When Knuzo found that his favourite snack of brown bread was no longer available, he was determined to find out what was happening to it, for the chef had gestured that he was still saving various items of food and leaving them on the ledge as usual.

Even before first light had begun to dissolve the mist of the early morning heat haze, Knuzo had positioned himself behind a mallow bush which was conveniently situated opposite the ledge of the kitchen window. When dawn just started to break, like cream dripping into a bowl of black coffee, he could see sufficiently well to detect the small bag of bread and fish heads on the ledge. Almost as soon as he saw it, the bag appeared to fall to the ground. Knuzo's large, saucer-like, bloodshot eyes searched the area beneath the shelf then, to his amazement, he saw a tortoise-shell cat with nervous-looking bright yellow eyes gather up the bag in its mouth and, with its head held high, it just managed to keep the bottom of the bag off the ground as it walked unsteadily away with its heavy bounty, heading west.

Although he could not move as silently as he would have wished, Knuzo was able to follow the burdened tortoise-shell cat on its journey down towards the sea. This was obviously one of Bethsheba's relatives, for it had all the characteristic markings of her tribe. Whenever the cat paused for an instant to put down the bag in order to pick it up again in a different grip, Knuzo stopped too, to nibble as nonchalantly as possible at some of the abundant wild herbs, for this was his idea of not giving himself away.

As daylight was now upon them, he recognised the tortoise-shell cat as Patachou, a male cousin of Bethsheba. By the time they had almost completed their descent to the coast, Patachou knew that he was being followed by Knuzo, but he decided that he would carry on as if he hadn't noticed a thing. Once he came adjacent to the bottom of the fine array of steps leading up to the chateau, he turned left to the chapel and disappeared from Knuzo's sight. Three minutes later, he reappeared without having the bag in his mouth and, taking a quick, nervous look in all directions, he ran like a cheetah back up the garden stairway in the direction of the mansion. Knuzo reflected upon this sudden turn of events, for he had expected to witness Patachou settling down in some secret hide to eat the fish heads and, perhaps, even leave the bread for him. However, in no way could the cat have devoured even one of the fish heads in the time he had disappeared from sight, so a puzzled Knuzo decided to investigate further and trotted up to the door of the chapel, which was slightly ajar, and pushed his way in.

Knuzo's rubbery nose, which gathered up smells like and industrial vacuum cleaner, could not help inhaling the odour of fish heads, although none could be found. However, it was in the far corner that he felt he came closer to them. Here, he found a small rectangular piece of mosaic work missing and, when he lowered his head so that his cave-like nostrils fitted over the gap, his lungs were immediately filled with the musty smell of bad fish. He raised his head quickly, his long ears falling back onto his unruly mane, and he brayed in disgust as he trotted, slipping as he went, quickly out of the chapel, to the fresh air of the outside world. What was one of Deputy Bethsheba's kinsmen doing, carrying the fish heads and his bread all the arduous way from the ledge by the chateau's kitchens down to the chapel, and then dropping them like a small parcel through a foul-smelling hole, situated in the far right corner of the old chapel's stone floor?

Fantasia had heard the noise of the donkey's hooves on the floor above the shaft, as well as a muffled bray. She had immediately run up the seven steps but, in spite of meowing, spitting, hissing and clawing at the dungeon's entrance, she had not managed to make herself heard. Exhausted and dejected, she fell backwards down the steps and, picking herself up at the bottom, she walked unsteadily to the sack, sat down and looked at the new pile of rations. She had found from past experience that some of the heads would be fresh, whilst others would be bad for, when Patachou dropped the food through the hole, some would become stuck in the crannies and were only dislodged at intervals when the next consignment came tumbling through it. The odour of bad fish mixed with the fusty warm air of the dungeon was building up to such an obnoxious level that Fantasia had to spend as much time as possible near to a ventilation hole which, due to the irregularities of the area, she had found the end on the seaward side of the tomb to be the best.

A further twenty-four hours went by and Knuzo's treat from the head chef disappeared once more and, although he was reluctant to get the tortoise-shell cat into trouble, he was beginning to miss his additional bread supply greatly and so he decided not to inform Nevasta direct but, instead, he waited for one of the oldest Senators, Dubnev, to take his almost daily ride on his back. The Senator, who was also possibly Nevasta's closest counsel, listened patiently to Knuzo's tale of woe and, when he reached the end of his description of the previous morning's events at the old chapel, he was quick to recognise that the tortoise-shell Patachou was involved in some type of clandestine operation. The old Senator slid off Knuzo's back and sped like a fresh breeze of wind through the shrubbery, past the towering Italian cypresses, and into the chateau. Some of the younger cats were astonished to see one of their oldest Senators moving so fleetly but, before they had time to gather their thoughts further, he disappeared up the grand staircase like a cannon-ball of fluff.

Dubnev collided with Nevasta just as he had reached the third floor, and the top cat, immediately sensing that something important was afoot, guided Dubnev into one of the turrets, where they could discuss whatever it was, in complete privacy.

Dubchev's chest was heaving in his attempts to regain his breath but he managed to divulge to Nevasta, through gasps, the important fact that for the last fifteen days Knuzo's daily gift from the head chef, of bread mixed with fish heads, had been disappearing and that, yesterday, one of Deputy Bethsheba's male relatives had been seen taking food to the chapel. Also, from the evidence presented, it looked very much as if the fish heads were being deposited by Patachou down a hole in the corner of the chapel.

Nevasta, like the born leader he was, was electrified into action. He ran into the corridor and along to the room which Fleur still used and, although not giving her a clue as to the reason, instructed her to locate, as quickly and as secretly as possible, the tortoise-shell Patachou, and to escort him to the turret with all speed. Fleur was pleased to be entrusted with such an errand, for the days had dragged like years since Fantasia's supposed drowning. Nevasta re-joined Dubnev, having first collected three more of his most trusted Senators. He quickly put them in the picture as to what had been related to him and briefed them on the roles they were to take when Patachou arrived in the turret.

After what appeared to Nevasta to be an eternity, the door was gently pushed open by Fleur who was followed by a very nervous and shifty-eyed Patachou. Nevasta was sitting on a high-backed chair, flanked on either side by two Senators and, as Patachou was ushered by Fleur to their leader, five sets of eyes immediately focused directly upon him and gave him the feeling that he was being devoured. Fleur withdrew from the room to wait outside the door. Neither Nevasta nor the Senators spoke a word but continued to stare directly at Patachou, which so unnerved the tortoise-shell that he found it difficult to stand properly, for his legs became as wobbly as jellies and he was too nervous to return any of their penetrating stares. He hung his head like a criminal who had been caught red-handed and immediately brought in front of a judge and jury. The silence in the room continued for a while until it was suddenly broken by Nevasta jumping down from his throne-like chair and snarling at Patachou, demanding to know to whom he was taking food down to at the chapel. This question was immediately repeated in unison by all four Senators, who almost unnerved themselves with the very intensity of their hissing.

Patachou, frightened out of his wits, flopped to the ground, his legs in disarray and his normally starch-like whiskers drooping like a flutter of flags being lowered at sunset. He confessed all, but made sure to stress that he had not been personally involved in the kidnap plot, nor the objective of getting rid of Fantasia. It had been Bethsheba who had master-minded Fantasia's kidnapping and imprisonment in the Abbot's grave under the chapel. Only three of Bethsheba's tribe of cats had been in on the actual kidnap, but all seven blood relatives had known about it and were sworn to secrecy. As far as Bethsheba was concerned, had not Nevasta met Fantasia, she would now be the most powerful and important queen cat in the kingdom. When she had seen the degree of

Nevasta's attention towards his pedigree guest, Bethsheba, filled with the blackness of intense jealousy, had poisoned the minds of her family about the evils of pedigree aristocrats and therefore how Fantasia must be got rid of at all costs, in order to safeguard what she termed the integrity and quality of life of the cat kingdom at Chateau Santa Sofia. Her relatives, the majority of whom relied on brawn and muscle rather than any degree of intelligence in order to progress, fell for Bethsheba's reasons for disposing of Fantasia and had carried out the kidnap and subsequent entombment on her behalf.

Bethsheba had been sufficiently cunning to not only ensure that she had taken no part in the kidnapping herself but, should the paw of suspicion be pointed at her, she had an irrefutable alibi; so, throughout the afternoon and evening of the banquet she had been helping various others in the vicinity of the dining room and kitchens. Obviously, it had entered Nevasta's mind that Bethsheba would have perhaps more of a motive to get rid of Fantasia than any other of his subjects, but every check on her had come back as empty as the police investigation in the neighbourhood had proved to be.

Patachou went on to tell Nevasta and the four Senators that, although he did not wish to be disloyal to his blood relatives, he could not bear to think of Fantasia dying from starvation in the dungeon-like room. Also, since a kitten, he had had half his tail missing and always been bullied and despised by his relatives, so he had become increasingly sensitive to the fate of others who were not in a position to stand up or fend for themselves. The opportunity to help another cat who had suffered at the paws of his selfish relatives had given him a great deal of pleasure, although he had not possessed the strength of character, nor was he sufficiently brave, to have reported to Nevasta the whereabouts of his pedigree guest.

Fleur was asked to take Patachou to her room and lock the door, whilst the four Senators followed Nevasta, at almost break-neck speed, down some flights of spiral steps leading directly from the turret to the ground floor. From the foot of the turret, Nevasta checked to see that the coast was clear, for he was anxious that no other members of his kingdom should see them on their mission, in case one of the kidnappers informed the jealous Bethsheba. When they moved across the gravel path, Dubnev had only just managed to pull himself out of a state of dizziness but, like the true old warrior he was, he mustered a further reserve of energy and managed to keep sight of Nevasta as he picked his way through a little known short cut down to the sea and the chapel.

The chapel door was ajar, as usual, and Nevasta sped across the mosaic floor like an Olympic skater and jumped on the abbot's tomb to the right of the altar. Patachou had told the party that he had overheard one of his uncles describe how the only way to gain access into the dungeon room beneath the tomb was by opening its wooden lid, and this was only possibly by putting all of one's weight on one of the wings of a celestial-looking cherub. When the right wing was bent down, the catch of the carved top sprang open and, with the aid of his four companions, the lid was heaved open.

Nevasta slid down the seven steps into the evil-smelling dungeon, where the obnoxious smell of bad fish made his stomach turn inside out and his eyes stream like waterfalls. At first, he found it difficult to see anything in the room, let alone Fantasia, for the contrast between the sunlight of the outside world and the nocturnal lighting of the dungeon was too great. Dubnev had managed to descend the stairs, but the atmosphere of the room had been too suffocating for such an elderly statesman and he just managed to climb out in time to recapture his breath and so prevent collapsing.

Not a movement in the dungeon was apparent and, apart from the pile of fish head evidence, Nevasta and his three companions began to think that they had been led on a wild goose chase, when he spotted the smokey-grey tufting of the underside of one of Fantasia's paws protruding from the sack. He carefully turned back the top of the nape of the sack to reveal the seemingly lifeless form of Fantasia. With the help of the Senators, the sack was successfully pulled away from her, whereupon the end of her tail was seen to twitch. There was life there, but for how long? The cat carrying drill was immediately put into effect, with two of them getting under Fantasia from opposite sides and when they stood up she was neatly supported on their backs. With Nevasta leading the way, and securing her gently by the neck, the third Senator took up the rear and, when they began to ascend the steep steps, struggled and pushed with all his might to keep Fantasia's back legs on the backs of his two colleagues whilst Nevasta, keeping his grasp of her neck, did all in his power to stop her from sliding backwards. Once the top had been gained, with a Herculean effort they hoisted her limp body over the side of the Abbot's tomb and onto the mosaic floor beneath. Before Nevasta allowed anybody to rest, Fantasia was carried out of the coolness of the chapel and laid gently on a cushion of moss that was bathed in sunshine.

Nevasta sat by Fantasia's head in order to shield it from the direct sun, whilst leaving the rest of her body to absorb the warmth of its rays, which acted like couriers of well-being, bringing her back to life. Her shoulders shuddered slightly, which seemed to set up a chain reaction within the rest of her body, for her tail twitched, her legs jerked and the now pale triangle of her nose forced out a cloud of the dungeon's rank smelling air. As the warmth of the sun worked wonders on restoring Fantasia's well-being, Nevasta's most trusted Senators recuperated from their exertions but, as she began to come round, they withdrew discreetly, not too far from but within easy call of their leader.

Fantasia flexed her legs and her claws came partially out of their ivory-white sheaths. As she arched her back, she passed her right paw over her right ear and then licked the inner side of the paw and repeated the process a few times before gradually opening her eyes completely. The first object she focused on was the proud, Olympian figure of Nevasta, whose large grey eyes were dancing with excitement, and his mind numbed with relief. His prayers to the oil mural of St. Francis of Assisi had been answered, his treasured guest had been brought back from the dead. In a fit of unabridged enthusiasm, Nevasta drew closer to Fantasia and rubbed his ginger forehead gently against hers. Fantasia's taut and somewhat emaciated body, the state of which well illustrated the ordeal she had just suffered, melted to within its wealth of now warm Persian fur. Her long dark eyelids fell like lace curtains, and her body vibrated to the harmony of the rhythm of their mutual purrs, before relapsing once more into a semi-conscious state.

Chapter Seven

An Aristocat's Dilemma

Half an hour later, Fantasia, who was still in the depths of sleep, had been placed on a silken-covered eiderdown brought down from the chateau, while Fleur had attended to her, rejoicing with every breath that Fantasia drew. Nevasta had despatched the youngest of the four Senators to act as courier and inform either the Count or Alexandre of Fantasia's rescue. Alexandre had come down from the chateau immediately, accompanied by one of the liveried valets. They were quick to gather up the eiderdown with Fantasia in its midst and to convey the precious bundle to the mansion and to her previous quarters there.

As the small party made their way up the wide garden steps, various members of the cat kingdom began to gather on either side of the balustrades, at first trying to determine whether their English guest had died or was still alive. However, it was the look of pleasure on their 'top cat's' broad face that conveyed to them the hoped-for information - the good news that, although Fantasia was at present in a state of collapse, she was expected to recover fully from her entombment, and such gratifying news spread ahead of them with the effectiveness of good tidings from a peal of church bells.

By the time the procession reached the shade of the group of red cedars at the top of the steps, there was an excited crowd of well over fifty purring cats, with Knuzo joining in the excitement by uttering a series of abrasive 'hee-haws', for the majority of the inhabitants of Chateau Santa Sophia had believed Fantasia to be dead. Even Caput, the tortoise, had got wind of the excellent news and was just in time to peer out of his shell to see for himself the return of the missing guest, for most of the cats had, during the past four weeks, spoken of little else apart from the nature of her disappearance. The only conspicuous absence from the congregation still running in from all sides, was that of the members of the tortoise-shell tribe and their leader, Deputy Bethsheba.

The news of Fantasia's re-appearance had been brought to Bethsheba as she, with her four murderous companions, were enjoying sadistic games with two 'eyed' lizards which they had cornered. On learning that Fantasia was still living, she broke out into a tirade of fury and abuse for, during the last ten days at least, she had felt confident that her rival had died of starvation in the Abbot's tomb - how could a cat possibly live in such conditions without so much as a morsel of food left for her? The more Bethsheba contemplated this aspect of her enemy's survival, the more she became certain that one of the seven tortoise-shell cats in the know had betrayed her and managed to get food to Fantasia. As Patachou was nowhere to be seen, and had been acting in a very strange manner lately, her suspicions fell on him.

Bethsheba stood with her back arched like a rainbow, her dorsal hairs standing on end like the stiff bristles of a toothbrush. She held her arrogant head high, her tail erect like a banner and, when she glanced in the direction of all the commotion near the red cedars, her cruel bottle-green eyes emitted undiluted expressions of pent-up jealousy and hatred. Her black lip curled into a snarl and, like an express engine letting off a burst of surplus steam, she spat out her vehemence. Then, with an air of contempt for the universe, accompanied by her four companions, she beat a hasty retreat for she realised, in her wisdom, that Nevasta would soon be sending out a search party to arrest her.

The tortoise-shell cats made use of a little known escape route and left the estate beyond the south lodge, where it was comparatively easy to climb a cypress tree, jump onto the top of the twelve foot high wall bordering the estate on the east side and down the other side onto the soft texture of the eucalyptus-lined minor road. Bethsheba and her companions were neither seen nor heard of again, although rumour did have it that they had crossed the border into Italy and were living a bandit-like existence in the hills behind San Remo.

Fantasia remained in a semi-coma for two days, with the ever-attentive Fleur plying her with warm milk and choice morsels of food whenever she awoke. The Count, Alexandre and Nevasta had visited her on several occasions. Initially, the Count had called in one of the top veterinary surgeons in the Cote d'Azur to check her over and to guide Fleur as to the type of food and nursing necessary to bring her back quickly to good health. The vet had told the Count that only a cat with iron-willed stamina would have been able to survive the kind of conditions and privations that Fantasia had experienced.

Nevasta hoped to himself that a least some of Fantasia's determination to survive was influenced by her care and admiration for him.

During Fantasia's forty-eight hours of twilight sleep, her mind was pulled to and fro like a tug of war, by the dilemma Nevasta had caused, in asking her to be his life-long companion. She kept thinking of what her pedigree relatives had brought her up to believe - that, as she was a member of a respected pedigree chinchilla Persian family, she was superior to the majority of other cats and, although it was important to make friends with other breeds (even cross-breeds), when having to choose a constant companion, only her own blue-blooded species should be considered. Although, to an outsider, this may appear to be a type of upper-class snobbery between pedigrees and pedigrees, and pedigrees and cross-breeds, it had been so deeply implanted in Fantasia's mind that, whenever her sentiments were about to be swamped by her wish to share Nevasta's life, such thoughts were soon reconsidered, due to her allegiance to her ancestors.

As the battle within her mind raged, Fantasia attempted to reconcile within herself what blue blood and pedigree status really represented and, during these thoughts, she reflected on the excellent values of the many different tribes of cross-breed cats at the chateau, which were often more deep-rooted and genuine than in the majority of their aristocratic counterparts. In whose eyes was she more respectable or respected if she confined having a long-standing companion to her own pedigree? As a pure chinchilla Persian, was she any better than a farm cat living at one of Parkington Hall's lodges? Why should she look down upon other cats who did not look as dignified as she, or who had not been initially as fortunate as

she, in being suckled and reared within the confines of the
Hall itself? Surely, a cat like herself should contribute more to
life than just resting on the laurels of her personal heritage?
She thought of the out-sized oil canvas of one of her ancestors
at Parkington, who was depicted so puffed up by her own self-
adopted importance. She reflected on her original intention to
grow up into a similar type of cat to that of her relative in the
picture, as well as on her ambition to have her master
commission a portrait of her to hang in a conspicuous place in
the hall, so that she, too, would be remembered for posterity.

Fantasia's mind sieved out the feline inequalities of
birthright and, as the mists of the coma began to lift, the dawn
of her new understanding of such values and life-style began
to materialise. When she had fully recovered and was able to
move from the silken eiderdown without having to be lifted,
she became ablaze with the joy of living, appreciating every
aspect of the daylight hours. The dramatic view from the
window of the cypress tree-clad landscape that fell away in a
tapestry of greens, all contrasted magnificently with the ever-
changing blues of the Mediterranean. The gentle blossom-
scented breezes, the caressing rays of the sun, the variety of
the food offered, the luxury of her quarters and, above all, the
friendship and concern for her welfare that had been showered
upon her, were all aspects of life which a cat, who had not
been subjected to the type of 'close to death' experience which
she had just had, would doubtless take so much for granted.

It was whilst Fantasia was in this state of re-discovered
euphoria and bonhomie that Nevasta again asked her to be his
life-long companion. Instead of falling into a deep slumber as
she had done on the previous occasion, she passed her
powderpuff-like right paw over her right ear, creasing the well

tufted ear as she did so, then licked the innerside of the paw and gently brushed her whiskers with it, with the skill of a beautician in a beauty parlour. Once this exercise was finished, she walked up to Nevasta and rubbed her silky forehead and her brick red nose against both of his cheeks and allowed, for the first time since their parting at Parkington Hall, the end of her tail to become momentarily entwined with that of his.

The news of such a future companionship swept through the chateau like a well-vented bush fire. The Count had taken them both to the state room and seemed to be equally as pleased about the news as Nevasta and Fantasia for, if the truth of the matter was known, the Count had always dreamt that one day he would bridge the gap between his kingdom of waifs and strays and true pedigree blood, leading to the desired classless feline society. Alexandre bent down to congratulate them both, whereupon the Count put around Fantasia's neck a regal purple collar, studded with rubies. For his 'top cat' he had a more masculine dark leather collar with a medallion dangling from it, bearing his familiar family crest partly occupied by the two stylish heraldic cats. The Count had sent a telegram to Lord Stocksfield as soon as he was sure that Fantasia would recover from her entombment under the chapel, and had now sent a second telegram with the news that their respective cats wished to remain together, at the same time urging his friend to travel down to Menton as soon as he was able, so that he could be present at the union, which the Count had vowed would be a celebration to beat all previous such occasions at the chateau.

The Count sent invitations to the owners of every well connected cat in the eastern part of the Cote d'Azur, and some went as far afield as Nice, Cros de Cagnes and Cap d'Antibes.

It was not that he wished either to influence or impress his cat kingdom with the presence of so many blue-blooded felines and their owners, but rather that he was more anxious to see whether those invited would be sufficiently tempted to accept the bait of having the opportunity to be present at the celebration of the union of a British aristocrat with his 'top cat', for invitations to previous functions had always been snubbed and gone unanswered. The Count felt confident that, if the majority of those asked did attend, they would have the opportunity to see for themselves the diverse quality, integrity and charm of the members of the chateau's cat population and that real friendship can break down all barriers, no matter how aristocratic and socially unjust these may be.

The first reply received was from the owner of the Siamese cat family, who was in turn acquainted with the sovereign Prince of Monaco himself. They resided close to the blancmange-pink palace which crowned the rock so clearly to be seen across the bay from the chateau. After news had got around that the well connected Siamese super cat of Monaco had accepted the Count's invitation, similar notes of acceptance were brought by the postman on his daily visit with almost the proliferation of a swarm of locusts.

Lord Stocksfield arrived a day before the feast was due to take place and this time, when Le Train Bleu steamed into Menton, he was met not only by the Count, Alexandre and Nevasta but also by Fantasia herself. His lordship, on seeing her, was immediately overwhelmed by his emotions and found it impossible to maintain his usual standards of British decorum and reserve. He knelt down on one knee on the station platform and rubbed Fantasia's chin on both sides with his knuckles, then gently stroked the silky dome of her head with the palm of his hand which Fantasia responded to with her most affectionate orchestration of purrs.

The feast of life companionship took place on a fine autumn day, such as only that particular region of the Mediterranean could boast. As the guests arrived, the dark green regimented columns of Italian cypress appeared to be standing more upright and uniform than ever before, acting as it were as nature's guard of honour. The Count's liveried valets guided the owners and custodians of their pedigree guests through the porch into the great hall and then, prior to allowing them to progress further, cunningly succeeded in mingling them with the chateau's hybrid residents. They were then directed into the state room where the pedigrees and the Count's kingdom of waifs and strays were split up into pairs for the duration of the celebration.

As the guests had entered the state room from the great hall they were able to look to their right and see, through the open double doors at the north end, the dancing waters of the marble fountain of Alambra; whereas, at the opposite end of the state room, to the south, the doors leading into the smaller room were also open. Everybody's gaze was directed towards the delicate cream alabaster mural of St. Francis of Assisi, which was lit from behind. The brown of the Saint's coarse robe, belted with a cord, contrasted magnificently with the snow-white purity of the doves that were illustrated circling about him or perched on his shoulder.

The lid of the concert grand piano was open and, standing within the graceful curve of its right side, were the Count, Lord Stocksfield and Alexandre. To the right of the humans was Knuzo the donkey, who was gallantly supporting on his armchair-like back Nevasta's oldest friend Dubnev. To the left of the Count, surveying the scene from the top of an ornate vase stand, was Caput the tortoise, flanked in turn by the now befriended Patachou who, in gratitude for his help to Fantasia, had recently been promoted to the rank of Deputy.

A sudden silence fell on all those assembled, when Nevasta and Fantasia appeared from a door opposite the grand piano.

Fantasia's chinchilla-grey long coat had bleached considerably since her arrival on the Cote d'Azur, but the magnificence of her thick fur and the way she carried herself with her bushy tail held erect like a banner, was sensational as she walked sedately, flanked on one side by the creamy short-furred Fleur and on the other side by the large, tiger-striped form of Nevasta, his various battle scars adding to the mystique of his warrior-like physique.

There were well over two hundred animals of all shapes, colours, markings, sizes, breeds, backgrounds and beliefs at this feast of union and friendship. The Count's cat dream had almost come true for, like St. Francis, he had always had a wonderful way with animals, in particular cats, and had striven all his life to bring a better understanding amongst humans and animals, as well as between animals themselves. The contrasting backgrounds of Nevasta and Fantasia being cast aside in this new era of understanding, mutual respect and friendship, which they now had for each other, represented the degree of goodwill upon which he hoped all future animal friendships would be based. The benevolence of St. Francis of Assisi had blessed all the residents and guests of the Chateau Santa Sophia that day, and it was, for the Count, the culmination of a lifelong ambition.

To Lord Stocksfield's Delight

Nevasta and Fantasia lived in the cats' dream world of Chateau Santa Sophia for some six more years and had one fine litter of three kittens; a son named Scobie and two daughters, Ninouska and Dubcek. Soon after the kittens were born, the Count died and, although Alexandre did everything in his power to persuade Nevasta to continue as his 'top cat', Nevasta decided to abdicate and hand over the reins of office to one of his most trusted friends, Senator Santos.

A tragedy had also occurred at Parkington Hall, for the still young Lady Stocksfield had been killed after a fall from her horse whilst out fox-hunting. Also, due to her great extravagances during her lifetime (the extent of which had only become fully evident after her death) Lord Stocksfield was obliged to mortgage his estate in order to pay his late wife's debts.

Once Scobie, Ninouska and Dubcek had become more independent of their parents, Nevasta in particular found the chateau too full of nostalgic memories of the Count to be really agreeable and, now that he had relinquished all of his 'top cat' duties, as well as no longer being required to instruct his kittens in the ways of survival and the art of living, he was anxious to live elsewhere. Alexandre, like his late uncle, was also blessed with the ability to understand the majority of the sentiments expressed by their cats and, as Nevasta and Fantasia had meant so much not only to his uncle but also to himself, he decided to accept an invitation from Lord Stocksfield to stay at Parkington Hall. Naturally, he took Nevasta and Fantasia too and, although Ninouska and Dubcek remained at the chateau, their eldest son, Scobie, was allowed to accompany them.

Until Fantasia's return to Parkington Hall, she had not fully realised how much the place had meant to her nor how much she had missed it. After Lady Stocksfield's accident, the wolf-hounds had been given to a laird in the highlands of Scotland, which enabled the three cats to take up residence in Fantasia's old quarters at the foot of the great carved staircase itself. Alexandre could soon see that Nevasta and Fantasia were revelling in the more tranquil surroundings of Parkington Hall and, due to this, he came to an arrangement with his uncle's old friend. However, before he left Parkington Hall he sent for Ninouska and Dubcek so that they, too, could join their parents and brother. He also sent for Fleur, who had been most upset at having to be separated from her mistress and companion, as well as not having the opportunity to visit Great Britain, the home of her Siamese mother.

It was after the arrival of the remaining members of Nevasta's family and their friend that Alexandre left Parkington Hall to return to the Cote d'Azur, and it was only then that Nevasta and Fantasia learnt what had transpired between him and Lord Stocksfield. In his will, the Count had left a very sizeable sum of money in order to look after Nevasta, Fantasia and their relatives. As Alexandre had concluded that Parkington Hall was more likely to provide a more satisfactory long-term environment for them than the Chateau Santa Sophia, he used part of the Count's legacy to pay off Lord Stocksfield's debts and, with the remainder, he entered into a gentleman's agreement which, as a mark of good faith, Lord Stocksfield insisted on having written into the deeds of his estate. This ensured that Nevasta, Fantasia and their descendants would have a rightful place as residents of Parkington Hall.

With the burden of Lady Stocksfield's sizeable debts lifted from his shoulders, his lordship was filled with gratitude and, to mark the occasion, he commissioned one of the most famous animal portrait painters in Great Britain to paint his beautiful Fantasia, who had helped - albeit inadvertently - to save his family estate. When the artist arrived at the Hall to undertake the work, Fantasia abandoned her lifelong ambition to have a portrait of herself depicted as a superior-looking aristocrat of a chinchilla Persian, on the lap of the Lord of the Manor, hanging in an ornate gilded frame next to one of her illustrious ancestors, peering down from the wall of the grand staircase. Instead, a portrait illustrating the cosmopolitan nature of her family was commissioned, in order to highlight just how the hybrid mix and blend between her blue-blooded aristocratic chinchilla Persian heritage with that of a most accomplished, yet self-made, charismatic ex-alley cat, represented the type of future that could only help to break down the social barriers and snobbishness between pedigree breeds and hybrids.

Thanks to the admirable examples provided by the union of Fantasia and Nevasta and the fine values demonstrated by their family life, the next generation of the Parkington Hall cat dynasty dedicated itself to do everything possible to bring about a fairer and more classless society within the cat kingdom.

THE END

ᵗhe United Kingdom
Source UK Ltd.
ᴖ001B/148-207